DATE DUE			
APR 04 2012			
JUN 21 2016			

THE ADVENTURES OF
BEANBOY

Written and illustrated by

LISA HARKRADER

Houghton Mifflin Books for Children
HOUGHTON MIFFLIN HARCOURT
Boston   New York   2012

Houghton Mifflin Books for Children is an imprint of Houghton Mifflin Harcourt Publishing Company.

www.hmhbooks.com

The text of this book is set in Glypha.

The illustrations are digital.

Library of Congress Cataloging-in-Publication Data

Harkrader, Lisa.

The adventures of Beanboy / by Lisa Harkrader.

p. cm.

Summary: Wheaton, Kansas seventh-grader Tucker MacBean loves comic books, so when his favorite comic has a contest to create a sidekick, he is hopeful that he can win, thereby fixing his struggling family.

ISBN 978-0-547-55078-7

[1. Family problems—Fiction. 2. Comic books, strips, etc.—Fiction. 3. Contests—Fiction. 4. Middle schools—Fiction. 5. Schools—Fiction.] I. Title.

PZ7.H22615Ad 2012

[Fic]—dc23

2011012161

Manufactured in the U.S.A.

DOC 10 9 8 7 6 5 4 3 2 1

4500337575

For my agent, Steven Chudney,
who recognized Sam Zawicki's potential
early on and never lost faith in her.
Thank you.

one

My best friend, Noah, was reading over my shoulder. "Weird how she's always got it in for little kids," he said.

"Yeah." I flipped the page.

Advertisement. Flipped again. Another ad. Flipped. Too many pages.

"You went past it," said Noah.

I flipped back.

Beep-beep. Beep-beep.

"Uh, Tucker?" Noah waved his wristwatch in my face. "Beecher's bus."

I tore my eyes from the blazing school building. Tried to focus on Noah's watch. He was still waving it around, so I couldn't see what time zone he had it set for, but I knew it was synchronized to the atomic clock at the Naval Observatory and updated continuously by satellite. When Noah's watch beeped, it wasn't kidding.

I smoothed *H2O Submerged, Episode Nine: Cataclysm* shut. Shot a glance at the back counter. If I was going to do this thing, I had to do it now.

Noah clicked his watch off and swung his bassoon case over his shoulder. Don't ask what a bassoon is. No one knows. I've been Noah's best friend since kindergarten, and I'm still not sure. It looks like . . . actually, it looks like Noah. Some people look like their dogs. Noah looks like his band instrument—skinny, perfect posture, shiny and dark.

I grabbed my backpack, and we threaded our way through aisles of comics, through the dust specks that floated on the few rays of light that had managed to beat their way inside. It had been raining all afternoon, and the damp air drew out the shop's wet-dog aroma.

We reached the counter, where Caveman sat hunkered over a graphic novel, his Hawaiian shirt stretched over the mountains of his shoulders, his wild black hair fluttering as he turned a page. He truly was a caveman. A caveman with a Wonder Woman lunchbox collection.

Case File:
Caveman

Status: Uncertain. (Hero? Unlikely. He's a little grumpy, but he doesn't fit the villain profile, either. And he doesn't like anybody enough to be their sidekick.)

Base: Caveman Comics

Superpower: The superhuman ability to know every single thing that is going on in his shop without ever paying attention to it.

Superweapon: Possibly an extra set of eyeballs concealed somewhere on his body. That would be my guess.

Real Name: Unknown. (I mean, no self-respecting parent actually names their kid Caveman. Do they?)

CASE FILE: INCOMPLETE

I pushed *H2O* toward him, reached into my shoe, and pulled out three dollars and twenty-one cents. I clanked it onto the counter. Caveman dinged the cash register open and slid the money in. He didn't even look at it. He knew I had the exact change. He slipped *H2O* into a plastic sack, handed me the receipt, and went back to his novel.

I swallowed. A nervous tang prickled my throat. I'd been working up my courage since Noah and I first stepped into Caveman Comics—no, before that, before we left school even—and if I didn't do it now, I wouldn't get another chance till next month.

Noah gave me an encouraging thumbs-up.

"So. Caveman." I slid the sack off the counter. Casually. You know, so it wouldn't look like I was making a big deal out of it or anything. "You ever think about deliveries?"

Caveman licked a finger. Turned a page. Didn't look up. "Nope."

At least, I think that's what he said. It was more of a grunt than an actual word. Which partially explains his name.

I took another breath. "It's just this idea I had. Deliveries, I mean. Like Pizza Rocket, only with comics instead of, you know, pizza. You should think about it."

Caveman turned another page. "Nope."

Nope, he wouldn't think about it? Or nope, he'd already thought about it, decided it was a bad idea, and was never going to think about it again?

Hard to tell.

"Okay." I nodded.

I tucked the receipt in my shoe (a.k.a. the best place

5

to store your most important paperwork), gripped the crinkly plastic stack, and started toward the door.

"Because here's what I was thinking," I said. Casually. Like I was tossing ideas at him on my way out. "It might do a lot for your business. You know, provide just one more service no other comic book shop provides."

Not that Caveman was big on service in the first place. But still.

"Dude." Another lick. Another page. "I'm not delivering your comic books. You can come down here and buy them like everybody else."

I stopped. A whole sentence. Two, actually.

"But see?" I said. "That's the beauty of it. These deliveries—they wouldn't be *to* me. They'd be *from* me. You'd hire me to be your comic book delivery man. On my bike."

With Beecher on the handlebars if I had to.

"Not happening."

I blinked. "Okay. But think about it because—"

"Not happening."

"Okay, but if you change your mind—"

"Tucker," Noah whispered. "I don't think it's happening."

I sighed. When Noah and I rule the world, comic book delivery will be mandatory.

Noah headed for the door. I trudged after him, the crinkly sack rustling against my leg. We wound our way through tables and racks and shelves, all groaning under the weight of the world's greatest superheroes: H2O and Batman, Superman and Spidey. American and Japanese.

We passed a small rack squeezed in between NEW RE-LEASES and GOLDEN AGE CLASSICS. One of Caveman's signs was thumbtacked above it, black marker on a scrap of dusty poster board:

LOCAL INDIES

Most people came in looking for the latest *X-Men* and didn't know these were here.

But I knew.

Because these weren't like the other comic books in the store. They weren't written by famous comic book writers and drawn by famous artists. They weren't printed in color on shiny paper and shipped out by the millions every month by Marvel or D.C. or Dark Overlord or some other behemoth comic book company.

Mostly they were black-and-white Xeroxes, carefully folded and stapled, printed a handful at a time, probably at the copy shop over by the university.

But they were here. Real live comics in a real live comic book store.

I pulled one out. Ran my hand over the grainy cover.

"So, hey. Caveman," I said.

He may have grunted. Or maybe not. The Cavester was a man of few words.

"Have these indie comics started making any money?" I said.

And sometimes no words. He didn't even glance up.

"Yeah. I know. Not as much as it costs the artists to print them. But I thought I'd ask. Just to see if anything had changed. I guess it hasn't."

I slid the comic back into the rack. Ran my hand over it one more time. One day that would be me. One day *my* comic books would be for sale. And not just here at Caveman. Across the country.

Across the country? Heck, around the planet. I'd be the most famous comic book artist ever, world-renowned for creating . . . well, I didn't know what. Yet. But he (or she—you can't be raised by my mother and not consider the very real possibility that the world's greatest superhero just might be a girl) would be amazing. The most amazing comic book hero ever.

I'd go to all the big comic book conventions, and the line of fans waiting for my autograph would stretch out of the building and around the block. Which would be exciting, but it wouldn't give me a big head. I'd still be humble. I'd still be Tucker MacBean from Wheaton, Kansas. I'd still talk to everyone who came up to me and thank them for the excellent things they said about my—

"Tucker." Noah tapped his watch.

"Yeah." I nodded. "I'm with you." I turned away from the indie rack. I'd have to be famous later.

Noah and his bassoon leaned into the glass door. The afternoon thunderstorm had fizzled out, but a leftover wind swirled in from the stairwell and spit drizzle at us.

I pulled the collar of my jacket up around my ears. Glanced back at Caveman.

"Thanks," I called back to him. "See you next month."

"I doubt it."

I doubt it? What did he mean? I was his most loyal customer. I bought at least one comic book a month. Every single month.

I was as dependable as Noah's watch.

And I told Caveman so.

"I always come in. The very day the new *H2O* hits the stands." Next month especially. The episode I held in my hand, *Episode Nine,* contained a secret that would rock the H2O universe. *Episode Ten* would be the epic show-down that changed that universe forever.

Caveman licked his finger and turned a page. "Yep."

That was all he said.

I shot a funny look at Noah, who was still standing in the doorway, the wind whipping specks of rain against his glasses.

"What does he mean?" I said.

Noah rolled his eyes. "Who *ever* knows what he means? Let's just go."

"It's got to mean *something*."

"Tucker? Hello? It's already"—Noah bent his elbow into a crisp ninety-degree angle so his watch was at eye level. He clicked through various cities (Tokyo, London, New York) till he finally got to us here in Wheaton—"three nineteen."

Case File:
The Spoonster

Status: Sidekick

Base: Basically, the Earhart Middle School band room

Superpower: Preventive action. (Noah always arrives early, always carries Kleenex, keeps four quarters, two spare pencils, an extra pair of gym shorts, and a tiny screwdriver—to fix his glasses and jimmy open my locker—in his bassoon case, and never leaves his homework till the last minute. Preventive action comes in handy more often than you'd think.)

Superweapon: His huge brain. (Noah is like the smartest kid ever. It's not his fault. His parents don't allow him to be stupid. They've enrolled him in every extracurricular activity invented, from music lessons to anthropology camp. Now he knows everything, including how to play ancient Korean folk tunes on the bassoon. Which goes over big in the seventh grade.)

Real Name: Noah Spooner

"Three nineteen? Why didn't you tell me?"

"I did. We're veering dangerously off schedule here. I have bassoon practice. And homework. And a firm bedtime. And if you miss Beecher's bus, your mom'll ground you."

"Ground me? Are you kidding?" I headed out the door. "If I miss Beecher's bus, she'll kill me."

"She'll kill you first. *Then* she'll ground you."

two

Caveman Comics lay halfway below street level, tucked beneath a bike shop and an Internet cafe. Steps led up from the door to the sidewalk, past the sputtering neon sign that flashed CAVEMAN, past the single dust-caked window carved into the bricks of Caveman's front wall. It really *was* a cave. A den. A secret hide-out for comic book geniuses like me and Noah.

Not a place for our arch nemesis.

But when we scuffed up the rain-soaked steps, there was Sam Zawicki: arms crossed, shoulders rigid, combat boot practically drumming a hole in the sidewalk.

And okay, so technically Sam Zawicki wasn't our *personal* arch nemesis. Technically, Sam Zawicki had way too much arch-nemesing power to waste on a couple of flyweights like me and Noah. Technically, Sam Zawicki

11

was too busy trying to arch-nemesis the entire seventh grade, most of Earhart Middle School, all of Wheaton, and, possibly, the universe.

Technically, Sam Zawicki was arch nemesis to the world.

She was standing in front of the display window of Weaver's Department Store on the corner, under the red canvas awning, a stream of rain dribbling off the canvas behind her. She was glaring at the mannequins in the display. Practically glaring a hole through the glass. Like she was itching for a fight. Like she was just waiting for those mannequins to start something. Like she was ready to take 'em down.

And I don't know if it was from Sam snorting her hot breath out into the damp air, or if it was just steam rising off her army surplus jacket, but her head—with the straggly brown hair and the chin jutting out—sort of rose from the fog that swirled around her.

Which, I have to admit, added a nice touch to the whole arch nemesis business.

She never really messed with me and Noah much as long as we stayed out of her way (except for one humiliating third grade bathroom incident that I don't really want to talk about).

This worked out pretty well for everybody, since staying out of the way was the main thing me and Noah were really excellent at.

See, Noah and I had developed the power of invis-

Good Super Villain Traits

sinister eyebrows
beady eyes
fiendish scowl

crooked nose
twirly mustache
pointy chin

steam
fog
patented Zawicki rage

ibility. The trick was to stay quiet, stay low, and not wear anything in the lavender, pink, or magenta color families. Invisibility could be lonely, but let's face it, when the third guy in your posse is a bassoon, it might just save your life.

"What are *you* looking at?" Sam Zawicki's croaky bark shot down Quincy Street.

I jumped. Because: 1) Sam Zawicki's voice is like a smack in the head, and 2) I realized I was staring at her. Or at least, staring at her reflection in the glass of the Weaver's Department Store display window, under the sign that said NEWLY ARRIVED! FALL DANCE DRESSES. I hadn't meant to, but there I was, staring Sam Zawicki in the eye.

And she was staring back.

She fired a look over her shoulder, past Weaver's, down the next block.

I glanced that way, too, to see what she was looking at. Probably her big lump of a brother, Dillon. He's not real bright, but when you're as big as Dillon, you don't need that many brain cells. But I didn't see him. Luckily. The whole Zawicki experience was miserable enough without throwing Dillon into the mix.

"Hey!" Sam's voice smacked me again. "Beanboy."

Yeah. Beanboy. It was the kind of thing you had to deal with when you were born with a last name like MacBean.

"Quit looking at me." She turned to face us.

"I wasn't. I just—"

"Quit following me. Quit breathing my air. You got that?" She pulled her backpack close and wrapped her arm around it, like she was guarding it.

From me, I guess. Like *I* was a big threat.

Sam was shorter than me, and her arms and legs were just plain spindly. Her combat boots were actually smaller than my sneakers. I'm no hulking maniac, but I hoped I at least *looked* like I could hold my own against a sixty-pound girl.

Right.

I took a step back. Her combat boots had steel toes.

Noah gave his watch a covert tap. I nodded and angled sideways, trying to dodge Sam and her boots.

She stepped in front of me, cutting me off.

"Look," I said. "I'm not following you. I do have to, you know, breathe, but I wasn't looking at you. I mean,

14

I *was,* but I didn't know it was you. I just thought you were, I don't know, some girl."

Sam stood very still. Which was somehow worse than when she was flinging her bony arms and snorting out arch-nemesis fog.

"Girl?" Sam's voice was low. "Did you call me a *girl?*"

"Uh—"

I cut a look at Noah, who raised his eyebrows in a kind of forehead shrug. What was the right answer here? I mean, she didn't act like a girl. She didn't walk like a girl or talk like a girl or dress like a girl or hit people like a girl. But technically she was, well, a girl.

"Um. Yes?" I said.

Sam narrowed her eyes. Opened her mouth to say something. Probably something I couldn't repeat out loud, in case my mother was listening.

But somewhere up the block, a bell jangled against a glass door. Sam stopped. Shot another glance over her shoulder.

I glanced, too.

"Stop it!" she barked. "Can you just for once stop being such a Beanboy?" She poked me in the chest. Hard. "Turn around, 'cause you're not going this way."

"But . . . I have to," I said. "My house is this way."

Probably not my best strategy. Tactical Tip of the Day: Never tell a Zawicki where you live.

She snorted arch-nemesis fog in my face. "Then you'll have to go around the block."

"Around the block? That doesn't even make—"

I was going to say "sense," but I never got a chance, because here's what she did next: She reached out and, before I knew what was happening, ripped the plastic sack from my hand. Flipped it like a Frisbee and sent it skittering behind me across the wet sidewalk.

It skidded over the concrete. Skidded over the cracks. Skidded smack into a puddle.

And for a second, it floated. For that short little second, Caveman's plastic sack kept *H2O* safe and dry. For a second, I had hope.

Till she ripped my backpack from my shoulder and

heaved it into the puddle. Splattered muddy water all over me and Noah. Crushed the sack and my comic book and my tiny bit of hope to the bottom of the puddle.

And I just stood there, frozen, and let her do it.

I'd spent my whole life thinking—hoping, dreaming, daring to believe—that no matter how gutless I appeared to the naked eye, no matter how . . . invisible, somewhere inside me, somewhere deep down where even I could barely find it, beat the heart of a superhero. And now, when I finally had a chance to prove it, when I could have stepped in and saved my comic book, could have stopped Sam Zawicki, could have finally become my true super-hero self, what did I do?

Nothing.

Not one dang thing.

I told myself it was because she caught me by sur-prise. Because I wasn't ready for her. I wasn't expect-ing her to be standing there on Quincy Street, and I sure wasn't expecting her to throw my comic book into a mud puddle. I mean, who expects that?

A superhero would. A superhero's lightning fast re-flexes would never become frozen by surprise.

I snapped out of my stupor and dragged my backpack and my comic book from the puddle. I shot a quick glance over my shoulder.

Sam was gone.

I scanned the street. Saw mostly college students.

Plus one rickety old guy carrying a rickety old paper bag out of the thrift shop, with something fluffy and pink billowing out the top.

But Sam Zawicki had vanished.

I poured a stream of water from my Caveman sack. Peeled my drowned comic book from the plastic and gave the soggy pages a flap. Stale, gritty puddle water flecked my face.

All I can say is, when Noah and I rule the world, comic books will be waterproof. Also fireproof, wrinkleproof, bulletproof, and stain resistant. But mainly waterproof.

Noah wiped the splatters from his glasses. "Beecher's bus'll be pulling up to your house in approximately"—he clicked his watch—"two point six minutes."

three

I left Noah and the bassoon wheezing on the sidewalk halfway to our house.

"Too bad you don't have your bike," he called after me.

Yeah. I sprinted through the rain and cold down Quincy Street.

Through the park.

Across the tennis court.

Hurdled the net.

More or less.

Okay, less.

Raced down Van Buren Street, sucking wind, the soggy comic book and its life-altering secret tucked under my arm.

The houses on my old street whipped past in a blur

of rain-soaked color: the dark red of Noah's front door, the yellow shutters of Emma Quinn's old house, the sturdy blue my mom had painted our house.

Well, the house that used to be our house. I ran my hand along the slick wet slats of the wooden fence as I hurtled past. Past the gate, the front walk, the orange in the tire swing—

Orange in the tire swing?

I swung around and jogged backwards, panting out white puffs of breath.

The tire swing was still there, right where it had always been, hanging from the gnarled oak where our dad hung it when Beecher was little. Only now it was planted with . . . flowers. A thick bunch of dark orange, kind of spiky, furry-looking . . . flowers.

Flowers in our tire swing. It was like another piece of our family had just peeled off and blown away.

I puffed down the street and through the alley. Popped out at the corner of Eighteenth and Polk. My house—the house where we lived now, or at least, some of us did— loomed out of the drizzle, two stories of ancient brick and curly white trim. By the time I stumbled into the yard, I was way past sucking air. I could taste my lungs in my throat. I bent over, hands on my knees, sweat steaming out of my hair.

And saw the back of the little yellow special-ed bus rumble off in a cloud of exhaust.

I straightened up. Spun around.

Waiting on our curb: nobody.

"Beech?"

I scanned the front yard. He had to be here. Somewhere. I couldn't lose him, too. The MacBeans were unraveling like a ball of twine. If I lost Beech, there'd be nothing left.

Nothing but me, and I'd be dead, because my mom would kill me.

I whirled around. Where *was* he? I was only a minute late. Two max. I slid my cell phone from my pocket to check. Okay, more like five or six. But still, where could the kid—

I spied the glow-in-the-dark Spidey backpack lying in the wet grass by the porch steps. A bony elbow in a red hoodie poked out from behind one of the big square porch posts.

"Beech. Man. You scared me."

"I know." My little brother leaped from behind the post, teeth bared, fingers gnarled into fake monster claws, glasses sliding halfway down his red nose. "I a monster. Rahhhrrrr." His roar hung on the chill air.

"You're a monster, all right." I snatched his backpack from the grass, climbed the steps, and pushed his glasses up.

He looked up at me, his hands still twisted into claws. "I hiding."

"I know. That's what scared me." I looked at him—hard. Tried to make my raspy voice sound serious. "What if I couldn't find you?" I waved my phone. "What if I had to call Mom?"

Beecher stared at my phone. "Tall Mom?" He has trouble with *c*'s. They come out sounding like *t*'s. "No tall Mom. I sorry." His claws drooped to his sides. "I want to be a surprise."

I let out a breath. "You don't have to be sorry. You're a really scary monster."

He glanced up. "Really?"

"Really."

I handed him his Spidey backpack. He started to wrestle the straps over his shoulders.

And spied the soggy comic book under my arm.

"Eight-two-oh!" His way of saying H2O. "New one?" He let his backpack drop to the porch. "Tool."

"Yeah. Well." I peeled the comic book from my armpit. "Not completely cool." I shook the pages. Dirty puddle water sprayed over both of us.

Beecher narrowed his eyes. "You drop it?"

"Yeah," I said. "I dropped it."

He nodded. Patted my arm. "No worry," he said. "I drop stuff, too."

He wrapped both hands around the front door knob and cranked it open. I picked up his backpack, pulled the mail out of our mailbox—the top one—and we thumped into the warm, dry entry hall.

Our house, like most of the old houses by the university, was split into apartments. One door opened onto narrow steps that teetered down to the basement, which our landlord called a cozy garden apartment, I called a festering sinkhole, and Rosalie, the music student who lived there, called the best she could afford on her pitiful scholarship budget.

Another door led to the first-floor apartment, where two astronomy students, Joe and Samir, lived with the pieces and parts of Larry, the enormous telescope they were building on the fire escape. My bike was parked by their door, a five-dollar bill tucked between the spokes of the front wheel. Besides my mom's car, my bike was our building's only transportation, and I was doing a pretty steady business renting it out on rainy days.

I unwound the money and tucked it in my jeans pocket. I'd put it in our jar later.

A wide staircase led up to our apartment, the whole second floor, tucked under the eaves. I hauled our backpacks up to the landing and collapsed. Beech sat down at the foot of the stairs and heaved himself up backward—*thump, thud-thud, thump, thud-thud*—one step after another. The kid doesn't have depth perception, which means he can't tell how far down is. Which means he's always afraid he's going to fall. It's not his fault. Something happened when he was born. He didn't get enough oxygen in his brain right at first. So he doesn't do everything the way everyone else does.

It's kind of embarrassing to watch a nine-year-old scoot up the steps butt first, but honestly, it's easier than trying to drag him up the normal way, his bony fingers clamped around my wrist, his fingernails dug into my veins, and his air-raid-siren voice screeching in my ear.

We didn't have this problem at our old house. Our old house didn't have steps.

When he finally reached the landing, I climbed the rest of the stairs and unlocked our door. I left it open, dropped our backpacks by the kitchen table, and peeled today's sticky note off the fridge. Mom had stuck it to the twenty-dollar bill under one of the fridge magnets.

HERE'S PIZZA MONEY. YOU KNOW WHAT TO DO. I CAN ALWAYS COUNT ON MY BOYS. LOVE YOU. MISS YOU. MOM

I was way too old to have my mom giving me love and kisses on a sticky note, but I was glad she put them on there. It made Beech feel better.

Mom wouldn't be home till after we went to bed. Since she'd gone back to college, she'd been more of a rumor than an actual person. She worked all day, went to class all evening, and studied all night. We *had* collected evidence of her: wet towels hanging in the bathroom, half-written term papers scattered across the kitchen table, clean socks that magically appeared in our underwear drawers while we were asleep. Plus our finely tuned MacBean Family Sticky Note System. So we were pretty sure she still existed. We were hoping that one day, when she graduated, she'd show up in three dimensions again.

I slid the money onto the counter by the phone. "You hungry?" I called to Beech.

He crawled through the door. Climbed to his feet. "Nope."

He backed the door shut and reached for the note. Ran a stubby finger over Mom's printing. He couldn't read, but he knew what the heart and the lips meant.

"Awww," he cooed at the note. "I love you, too."

He kissed it, then stuck it by the phone, next to the twenty-dollar bill.

He poked at the rumpled mess of a comic book. "This."

I looked at it. The big secret that would forever change H2O's universe was right here in my hand. And it was too wet to read.

I sighed. "We have to let it dry first. Don't make that face. I want to read it as much as you do. More, probably. But look—the pages are all stuck together. You don't want to mess it up, do you?"

He frowned. "You already mess up."

Well, yeah.

"Here, I'll set it by the radiator." I propped *H2O*, pages fanned out, beside the rattling beast under our fogged-up window. "See? It'll be dry pretty soon. While we're waiting, I can make pancakes."

That caught his attention. For about a nanosecond. "Bear?"

I nodded.

He considered this. Then the nanosecond was over. "Nope."

"But you love teddy bear pancakes."

"Nope."

"If we have pancakes, we can save the pizza money and put it in the jar."

That stopped him again. For a fraction of a nanosecond.

Then he knelt down beside the radiator. Pointed at $H2O$. "This."

He looked up at me with his cockeyed, scrunched-nose squint. I'm sure he looked all cute and innocent to the unsuspecting bystander, but I had experience with that squint—nine long years of experience—and there was nothing innocent about it. That squint meant Beecher MacBean was locked onto $H2O$ like a fighter jet locked onto its target, and there wasn't enough pancake syrup in the world to pry him loose.

"Fine." I gathered up $H2O$. "Let's go read a wet comic book."

Beecher climbed to his feet. "Tool."

four

Case File: H2O

Status: Superhero

Base: A secret laboratory in the North Atlantic

Superpower: A freak accident changed the molecular structure of his body so that he is now 100% water. For most people, this would be a real bummer, and H2O does experience dark moments of soul-searching despair (dark moments of soul-searching despair are pretty much a standard requirement in a superhero), but he's learned to harness his waterpower into superhuman strength, speed, and vision.

Superweapon: Physics, pure and simple. He possesses all the properties of water, including the ability to exist in three separate states of matter. Mastery of physics comes in handy when you're fighting a mad scientist over control of the known universe.

Real Name: Marcus Poole, founder of NAUTICA Enterprises

Beech and I perched on the edge of the tub, damp towels hanging over the shower rod above our heads. The left-over scent of Mom's mango shampoo wafted around us.

I turned Mom's blow dryer to low and trained it on the *H2O* cover.

"More." Beech grabbed the dryer and flipped the switch to high.

The dryer roared. Wet pages whipped about.

"Hey!"

I wrangled the dryer from his hands. Smoothed out

H2O. The cover was torn. Pages were coming loose from the staples.

"I sorry." Beech shrank back onto the edge of the tub and clasped his hands together in his lap. He leaned against me. "Hurry," he whispered.

I turned the dryer to low and blew the page dry.

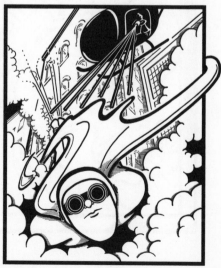

Beech touched the page. "Dry." He flipped it over and pointed. "More."

I trained the dryer on the next soggy page.

Madame Fury's laser flashed from red to ice white and split into six beams, each shooting toward H2O like a

missile, freezing him on contact. H2O struggled to reach the school.

I peeled the next page free. Beecher bounced up and down on the edge of the tub.

He grabbed my arm and gave it a squeeze. "You rot."

H2O stretched his frozen body toward the burning roof. Flames licked his fingertips. His hands melted and dripped onto the school in a steaming hiss.

"Uh-oh." Beecher poked a finger at the damp page.

"It's okay." I held the blow dryer steady. "H2O can handle it."

Yeah, he'd lost a hand. Major problem for a standard human being like me or Noah. But H2O could freeze, melt, evaporate, condense—in pieces or as a unit—then reassemble his particles and return to his normal liquid self. It sapped his strength for a while, but eventually he recovered. It was one of the perks of being composed entirely of water.

I turned the page and aimed the blow dryer.

Okay, *that* was a problem. H2O remained suspended by the freeze beam. The molecules of his hand—now a wisp of steam—drifted toward the stratosphere, while his arm was trapped as liquid in Madame Fury's lab flask. Hard to reconstitute yourself when your body parts were in three different places, in three different states of matter, with one of those states floating through the atmosphere as water vapor, restoring itself who knew where— a river, a pond, possibly a toilet bowl.

But H2O had been in tough spots before. He'd been diluted. He'd been polluted. He'd been sealed into a giant Ziploc bag and anchored under the polar ice cap.

And just when you were sure he'd finally met his end, he reached deep within himself, pulled out previously un-

tapped reservoirs of strength and courage, and thundered back, more powerful than ever.

I smoothed the page over. Advertisement. Peeled the next soggy page free. Another ad. And another. Then the back cover: ad.

I stared at the comic book. That was it? That was how *Episode Nine* ended? What about the big secret? The explosive development that would rock the Overlord universe?

I flipped back. Maybe I'd lost a page when it skidded into the puddle. I didn't remember one tearing loose, but with Sam Zawicki around, it was hard to keep track. Things happened fast. I flipped back again.

Every page: damp, wrinkly, hanging on by one staple, but present and accounted for.

Beecher, his face scrunched in confusion, looked up. "More?"

I rifled through to the first ad.

And that's when I saw it. It wasn't an ad at all. It was put in by the Dark Overlord comic book company itself.

Beecher jiggled my arm. "Read."

Will H2O escape? It's up to you. Until now, H2O has battled alone, alienated by his freakishly aqueous body, unwilling to let anyone get close.

But a lone warrior is a vulnerable warrior. And this time, H2O needs help. Without it, he will not be able to save himself or Planet Earth from Madame Fury's vengeance.

Will H2O—and ultimately the planet—survive? The answer depends on you.

Me? If the planet depended on me, Earthlings were in big trouble.

H2O—and the *H2O Submerged* series—cannot continue without your help. To save H2O, create an original superhero sidekick.

H2O's sidekick must possess the true heart of a hero. Reach deep within yourself, find that heroic heart, and create a sidekick who can rank among the greatest sidekicks in comic book history.

The winning sidekick will become H2O's partner against crime in all future H2O episodes, beginning with the final episode of the *H2O Submerged* series, which will be published—

Published. Like a real comic book. That people would read. Not just people here in Wheaton. People across the country. Across the country? Heck, around the planet.

—which will be published next year.

Huh. So that's what Caveman was grunting about. I couldn't come in to buy *H2O* next month because there wouldn't *be* an *H2O* next month.

The winner of the contest will receive a full college scholarship.

College scholarship? I blinked. One thing we could use around here was a college scholarship.

five

I didn't need a college scholarship.

Eventually I would need one. But not for another six years, assuming I survived middle school and high school.

The person who needed a scholarship—immediately—was my mother. With a scholarship, she could quit her job at the bank (the whole reason she'd gone back to college in the first place), go to school during the day (like a normal person), be here at night to order our pizza and make sure Beecher brushed his teeth (more of a bonus for me than for her), and actually get a decent night's sleep once in a while (because really, besides vampires—and Batman—who stays awake that many nights in a row?).

I don't know why I never thought of it before, especially with Rosalie and her pitiful scholarship budget living two stairways below us. A scholarship could be the answer to everything. So many pieces of our family had been peeling off and spinning into space lately. Dad only existed in e-mails. Mom wasn't much more than a sticky note. And now somebody had planted flowers in our tire swing. It felt like one day we were just going to spin away into nothing. And no matter what I did, I couldn't catch the pieces as they flew by.

Until now.

I ordered a large cheese pizza, with just enough pepperoni slices to make a happy face: two for the eyes, one for the nose, a row of slices for the mouth. Luckily, we'd ordered enough pizza that Pizza Rocket didn't even ask anymore. As soon as they saw our number on caller ID, they started lining up the pepperoni. I dispatched Beech to the kitchen to wait for the delivery guy and carried *H2O* down the hall to my room.

My room, a.k.a. the Batcave.

Outside, the streetlight cast a foggy yellow glow. Wind rattled the windows. Rain snaked down the glass. Out there, the world was cold, gray, a little dangerous. But here, inside, my room was like a fortress: snug, dry, sealed away from danger.

My H2O action figure gazed down on me, his Genuine Crystal-Luxe muscles flexed, ready to blast any slimeball who dared infiltrate the Batcave.

I checked my text messages, not expecting to

find much, except maybe from Noah, covertly sent between homework, bassoon practice, and whatever brain-enlarging extracurricular activities his parents had signed him up for this week.

Nothing.

I fired up my computer and found an e-mail from my dad. Which I kind of wanted to open (because it was from my dad) and kind of didn't (because it was from my dad).

Because here's the thing about my dad: He hardly ever e-mails, and when he does, it's not just to check in and see how we're doing or to tell us what the weather's like in Boston or to forward some stupid Internet joke.

No.

My dad e-mails when he has Something on His Mind.

I clicked OPEN.

Tucker,
What's this about wanting money for your birthday instead of a gift? Is your mother having some kind of financial crisis? Because if she is, she needs to take care of it herself. She shouldn't expect you boys to give up your birthday gifts. Don't worry. This isn't something you need to concern yourself with. I'll call and straighten her out.

Call her?
NO.
No, no, no, no, no.

That wasn't how it was supposed to go.

How it was supposed to go was:

1. Dad opens e-mail from me.
2. Dad thinks: *Great! Now I know exactly what to give my son, and it won't even cost that much to mail.*
3. Dad sends money.

That was the plan.

It was a simple plan.

Can't anyone follow a plan?

He's my dad and everything, so I would never say this to him, and I feel bad even thinking it, but if he would've just followed the main plan in the first place, and stayed here in Wheaton instead of taking his big hot job in Boston, and if he and Mom would've figured out how to stay married to each other, we wouldn't even be having this conversation.

We for sure wouldn't be having it in an e-mail.

My fingers started typing.

Dad,

No need to call. Seriously. Mom's fine. We're all fine. No financial crisis here. I only asked for money because I thought it would be easier. Because of how busy you are. And because last year you said the cost of postage was getting out of hand, and the post office was robbing you blind. But if you want to go shopping, that's fine. Great, in fact. But you don't need to call Mom. Really.

Tucker

I hit SEND, transmitted a few brain waves along with it to help convince my dad, then reached into the dusty space behind my monitor. In the back, hidden under an old H2O poster, sat our pickle jar. I lifted it out and gave it a swirl. Dollar bills swished around the pennies, nickels, dimes, and occasional quarters that jingled in the bottom.

← Former pickle jar

MOM'S CRUDDY JOB SAVINGS BANK

lonely quarter →

Ever since Mom started back to school, Beech and I had been saving our leftover pizza money—plus my bike rental fees and our recycled pop can earnings and the change Beecher dug out of the coin return slots at the

Laundromat—and stashing it all in the jar. Every time I plunked money in, I recorded it on a sheet of paper I'd taped to the front. Our goal: Save enough money for Mom to quit her job.

If Caveman would've gone along with my comic book delivery plan, I could've added my earnings to the jar.

If my dad would've gone along with the birthday money plan, I could've put that money in, too.

And that would've been a lot. A *lot*, a lot. Because I knew what he was going to get me. The same thing he always got me: a baseball bat. A really expensive big-barrel aluminum alloy bat. To replace the really expensive big-barrel aluminum alloy bat he sent last year and said I'd probably outgrown.

(Which I may have. How do you know when you've outgrown a bat? Luckily, my dad knew. For him, I think the bats were like magic beans. He was hoping if he kept sending them, maybe one day he'd look out his window and see that I'd sprouted into an athlete.)

I rubbed my thumb over the paper. Grand total so far: $48.63. I sighed. Forty-eight dollars and sixty-three cents didn't make much of a rattle in a gallon-sized pickle jar. It sure didn't rattle enough for Mom to quit her job. It barely rattled enough for her to take an afternoon off.

Beecher tottered in balancing the pizza box, the change from the twenty-dollar bill wadded in his bony fist. He set the pizza on my bed and handed me the money— four crumpled dollar bills and a handful of change. I plunked it into the jar along with the five dollars I'd retrieved from the spokes on my bike and added the new total to the paper: $58.38.

Beecher watched, his face rumpled in a hopeful scrunch. "Mom no tuddy job now?"

I shook my head. "Not even close, Beech-man."

"Oh." His shoulders slumped.

"Don't worry." I gave Beech a little punch in the arm. "I have a plan."

He looked up. "Really?"

"Really."

Beech burrowed down on my bed, opened the pizza box, and spun it around till the happy face was turned the right way. He couldn't eat if the face was upside down.

I slid the jar back behind my computer and covered it with the poster, rubbed H2O's Genuine Crystal-Luxe head for luck, and burrowed down into my desk chair.

I couldn't protect mankind. I couldn't defend the planet. I couldn't even save my own comic book from Sam Zawicki. But create a kick-butt assistant for the world's greatest superhero? This I could do. This I was *born* to do.

And I wouldn't have to Xerox my black-and-white drawings at the copy shop and beg Caveman to put them in the INDIE section of his store. If I did this right, if I created the best superhero sidekick the Overlord universe had ever seen, I could be in comic book stores everywhere. In full, glossy color.

My mom would have a scholarship. Beecher wouldn't have to get his kisses from a sticky note.

And I'd have fans. Millions of fans, across the country. Heck, around the world.

Maybe even at my own school.

I stared at *Episode Nine*. At my own school. Wouldn't that be . . . weird?

Because, let's face it, up to this point I hadn't exactly been winning the popularity wars at Earhart Middle. I wasn't a complete dork. I don't think anyone actively hated me (except now, suddenly, Sam Zawicki, but she hated everyone). I was pretty much known as the kid with the comic books, and on the sliding scale of middle-school coolness, comic book obsession hovered somewhere between geography club and the math team. It wasn't social suicide like, say, chronic B.O. But it sure didn't lift me up to the ranks of the basketball team's starting five.

But what if it could?

I opened *Episode Nine* to the contest and read through the instructions once more, careful not to miss any rule or requirement that would get me disqualified.

Entry had to be postmarked by midnight, October 15—check.

Judges' decisions were final—check.

Winner authorized Dark Overlord, Inc., to publish the winning entry in comic book form—well yeah, that was the whole point, duh, check.

Prize couldn't be redeemed for cash—bummer, but okay, check.

And then the final rule. I read it. And stopped dead in my desk chair.

This prize is nontransferable.

Nontransferable. Meaning . . . what?

I looked it up in my handy desktop dictionary.

nontransferable (adj.): not able to be transferred.

For a reference book, dictionaries seemed to go way out of their way not to include much reference.

But I had something way more reliable than a dictionary. I turned back to my computer. This was too big to fit in a text message.

To: BassoonMaster
From: SuperTuck
Subject: Hypothetical Question

Noah,
What if I entered a contest and wanted to give the prize to, say, my mother. But what if the contest rules said the prize was "nontransferable." What would that mean?
Tucker

I clicked SEND, then gnawed on a slice of pizza till my computer dinged.

To: SuperTuck
From: BassoonMaster
Re: Hypothetical Question

Tuck,
I don't know what you're doing, but if a prize is non-transferable, it's yours. Your mom can't have it.
Noah

I slumped in my chair.

The MacBeans were right back where we started: recycling pop cans and scrounging Laundromat change.

six

I lumbered beside Beecher, who stumbled beside Mom, who was finally more than a sticky note. It was early Sunday, so early, morning fog still snaked along the wet grass at our feet.

So early, my eyes were barely open. But I didn't care. We had Mom here with us finally.

Bonus #1: She wasn't hunched over the kitchen table, reading a fifty-pound textbook.

Bonus #2: We weren't hauling a month's worth of dirty clothes to the Laundromat.

We were almost like a normal family.

"I hungry." Beecher's voice drifted out from behind his pumpkin.

He'd fallen in love with a pumpkin the size of a mini-van at the first stand we passed. And even though he could barely reach his arms around it, even though it was the most lopsided, ugly pumpkin ever grown, even though Halloween was more than a month away, no way was he leaving the Wheaton Farmers' Market without it.

My job was to make sure it didn't die a gooey death on the pavement.

I sneaked a glance at Mom. Her face glowed pink in the chill of the morning. The usual knot of worry between her eyebrows had smoothed out into regular skin. She sucked in a deep breath of crisp farmers' market air, and the corners of her mouth curled up in an almost smile.

She never looked like that at the Laundromat.

"I *hungry*," Beecher said again.

"Shhh." I flicked him on the head. "Mom's happy. Don't ruin it."

"I no ruin it."

"Ruin what?" Mom smoothed her hand over his hair. "You couldn't ruin anything, Beech-man."

Huh. She had clearly not spent enough time with him lately.

She looped her hand around Beecher's shoulders, and he sort of leaned into her and buried his face in her jacket. And that's how we threaded our way through the crowd: Mom clutching her yellow sticky note, Beech and the pumpkin sort of stuck to her rib cage, me gimping along beside, one hand hovering under the pumpkin, ready to save its life.

A wave of warm, sweet doughnut aroma floated on the morning air. My stomach growled.

But Mom pushed on. Doughnuts were not on her sticky note.

First thing this morning Mom had tossed an empty cereal box in the garbage and caught sight of the other trash stuffed in there.

"Is this what we eat?" She picked through macaroni boxes, frozen waffle boxes, syrup bottles. I think it was the microwave corn dog wrappers that finally tipped her over the edge. "It's all starchy and mushy and"—she frowned—"beige."

Well, *yeah*. Meet Beecher MacBean, who only eats if his food is beige. With a face on it.

Mom decided on the spot that what our family needed—immediately—was vegetables.

Now we were winding our way through stands of veggies, fruit, organic honey, and handcrafted soap. Finally, at the end of the very last aisle, Mom stopped. She checked her sticky note, tucked it into the pocket of her jean jacket, and planted herself in front of a stand.

I *guess* it was a stand. Mostly it was rickety pickup truck, more rust than paint, backed up at the end of the row. Cardboard boxes, held together with duct tape and piled high with vegetables, filled the tailgate. An old man, rickety as his truck, leaned against the fender. White stuffing wisped out from the lining of his jacket. White hair wisped up from his skull. Duct tape held the toe of one work boot together, and white socks leaked out from the cracks.

Nothing about this outfit said healthy to me, but Mom had consulted an expert—Rosalie, our downstairs music student, who was really big into all-natural stuff—who said this stand sold the best vegetables in the market.

It did have a pretty good crowd clustered around it, picking through shiny red apples and fat potatoes and onions. The white-haired man watched over his veggies like a proud parent. I squinted. Somehow he looked familiar.

Mom stood with her hands on her hips, studying the duct-taped boxes. She furrowed her eyebrows. Probably it had been so long since she'd seen an actual vegetable, she wasn't sure what she was looking at.

I helped Beech lower his lopsided pumpkin to the ground and propped it up with my foot.

Mom reached into a box and wrestled out something round, bulging, and suspiciously purple. "So." She held it up. "What do you think?"

I stared at it. "Is that a . . . beet?"

"Hey, mister." She aimed the purple thing at me. "Beets are highly nutritious. Packed with vitamins. And beta carotene. One thing we could definitely use more of is beta carotene."

I didn't want to hurt her feelings, but . . . "A beet?"

"And fiber. Amazing amounts of fiber. And it's not beige. You really can't go wrong with a colorful root vegetable. It's the whole package."

"Uh-huh," I said.

"Not doughnut," Beech muttered.

Mom studied the beet, then, with a sigh, set it back. "You're right."

She studied the rickety truck. And decided to take the safe route: apples.

"At least it's something we know how to eat," she said.

As the man bagged our apples, he noticed Beecher crouched beside the pumpkin.

"You got a load there, don't you, fella?" he said. "Maybe I can help. Hang on a minute."

The man disappeared around the side of the truck. When he came back, he was pulling a little red wagon. At least, it used to be a little red wagon. Now it was a little rust wagon, the handle bent, the Radio Flyer emblem a ghost against the corroded metal. But the wheels moved right along, without a squeak.

The man wheeled it to a stop beside Beecher, lifted the pumpkin into the back, and set the bag of apples behind it to keep it from rolling over. He placed the handle in Beecher's palm.

"Now you can drive that pumpkin of yours around in style." He gave the lopsided pumpkin an admiring look. "It sure is a beauty."

"Yep." Beech ran a hand over the nubbly pumpkin. "Beauty." He beamed up at the man.

Mom did, too. "We'll haul the pumpkin to the car and bring the wagon right back."

The man waved a work-browned hand at her. "No hurry."

We rumbled off, Beech pulling the wagon with both hands, the pumpkin and bag of apples bumping along in the back, me making sure they didn't bump out onto the pavement.

We made it to the parking lot, and while Mom unloaded the apples into our car, I braced the wagon so it wouldn't roll away. My nostrils drifted in the direction of the doughnut stand—

—and I found myself, once again, staring straight into the eyes of Sam Zawicki.

She was marching across the parking lot toward us, feet pounding so hard I swear she left boot prints in the asphalt. She thumped to a stop, cut a look at my mother's legs (half dangling from the back seat as she wrestled Beecher's pumpkin into a seat belt), and held out a bony hand.

"Give it," she snarled.

I took a step back. "What?"

Sam rolled her eyes toward the sky. "The wagon, Beanboy."

The *wagon?*

"No." I pulled the handle closer, suddenly feeling protective of our rickety, rusty pumpkin-mobile. I squared my shoulders. "We promised to take it back."

Sam leaned in till we were practically nose to nose.

"I said, *give* it." She ripped the handle from my hand.

Which just made me mad. What kind of person steals a wagon? From an old man? She couldn't *want* the tumble-down thing. Or need it. She was taking it out of pure meanness.

But we were talking about Sam Zawicki here, the girl who once dumped Spencer Osterholtz's lunch tray into his lap when he said his carrot sticks were squishy. Who gets that worked up over a carrot?

No. The big surprise wasn't that Sam Zawicki was stealing a wagon. The big surprise was that she wasn't any good at it. I mean, if you would've asked me who, of all the people at Earhart Middle, would make the best wagon thief, I would've said, "Sam Zawicki."

But now here she was, right out in the open, swiping a wagon in a public parking lot. From me, the one person who could identify the culprit. A pretty pathetic start to her criminal career.

But she didn't look pathetic. She looked like she always looked: crackling mad.

She speared me with a Zawicki Glare of Death, then turned to go, rusty wagon handle gripped in her white-knuckled hand.

This was my moment, I realized. The moment I could reach inside and find my superhero heart. The moment I could stand up for truth, justice, and rusty wagons everywhere.

I swallowed, opened my mouth, and—

"Well, hi there."

My mother had finished buckling the pumpkin and was now looking at Sam. Wearing her how-lovely-to-meet-you smile.

I closed my eyes. I knew that smile. Things could only spiral downhill from here.

"I don't think we've met before. Tucker, why don't you introduce me to your friend?"

Friend?

Friend?

I sincerely think I lost consciousness for a moment, right there in the parking lot. It was almost as humiliating as the third grade bathroom incident.

Sam Zawicki gaped at my mother in pure horror. "No. I'm—I'm"—she edged backward—"just here for the wagon."

"Well. Isn't that sweet?" Mom unzipped her purse.

Sweet? I stared at my mother. She was clearly more vitamin-deficient than I had realized.

Because here's what she did next. She reached into her purse and pulled out a dollar. A real live actual dollar bill that could have been put to good use in our pickle jar.

But did she put it to good use? No. You know what she did?

She held it out toward Sam. Sam *Zawicki*. And said, "Such a thoughtful deed deserves a reward."

I froze.

No way.

No.

Way.

First of all, who uses the word "deed" besides my mother? And possibly the Cub Scouts?

And second of all, Sam Zawicki was stealing a wagon right out from under our very noses, and my mother was paying her to do it.

I love my mother, but I do not know what planet she's from.

Then I heard Sam say, "No. Really. No." She backed away from my mother's dollar like it was radioactive. "I couldn't."

My mom shrugged. "Well, thank you anyway." She tucked the dollar back into her purse. "You saved us a trip back to the stand."

Oh, sure. And saved that farmer from having to pack the wagon up and take it home again where it belonged. Just liberated him from that whole responsibility.

Sam and the wagon rattled away. I stood there and watched. Me and my superhero heart.

Mom shut the car door, I pushed Beecher's glasses up, and—

Dun. Dun. Dun. Dun duh-dun, duh-dun, duh-dun.

Beech froze. I froze. Even Mom froze for a tiny second.

It was the Death March, blaring from Mom's purse, and don't tell her boss, but that's the ringtone she programmed to go off only when *he* called.

Mom closed her eyes. The little knot of worry popped up between her eyebrows.

Don't answer. I beamed brainwaves at her. *Don't answer, don't answer, don't answer.*

She dug her phone from her purse, flipped it open, and turned her back so she could talk.

Beech looked up at me. "Bad news?"

I shrugged, like I didn't know. But I knew.

Mom flipped her phone shut and turned to us, a pained smile plastered across her face.

"You have to go to work?" I said.

She nodded.

"No." Beech's fists clenched at his side. "Day off. You promise."

"I know, Beech-man." She pulled him to her side. Ran a hand through his hair. "But something came up, and they need me."

"You work all the time," I said. "Can't they get somebody else?"

"I wish."

Mom opened the car door again and strapped Beecher in the back.

He slumped against the pumpkin. "Bad news," he told it. "Real big bad news."

seven

Mom drove me and Beech home.

"I'll be back as soon as I can." She unbuckled Beech. "If I get home early enough, we can still do something this afternoon."

Beech perked up. "Really?"

Mom nodded. "Really."

She sputtered off to work. Beech and I wrestled the pumpkin and the apples up to our apartment.

Beech climbed up to the living room window. Scanned the street below for Mom's car.

"Beech. Dude. She's not going to be home for a while," I said. "Plus you're wrinkling the curtains."

I turned to the cartoon channel. Sat Beech on the couch and tried to watch TV with him. Glanced out at the empty street. Wandered back to my room. Thought about doing my math homework. Thankfully, that thought passed pretty quickly. Wandered back to the living room.

Still no Mom.

I slumped onto the couch. Pulled the fuzzy throw over my shoulders.

The MacBean Family Apartment was pretty much empty most of the time, with just me and Beech and a couple sticky notes rattling around. And we were used to it. Mostly.

But now, today, knowing that Mom was supposed to be here, the whole apartment seemed . . . hollow.

My cell phone jangled.

It was Mom.

"Hey, Tuck." Her voice sounded really tired.

"Hey, Mom."

"Mom!" Beech clamped his jabby little fingers around my arm. Tried to wrestle the phone away.

"Stop it," I hissed. I wrangled my arm back.

"Bad news, buddy," Mom was saying.

I swallowed.

Beech pushed his ear to the phone.

"We've got a mess here." Her sigh floated through the line. "The computers went down, and we just now got them back up. I've got a ton of work."

I nodded, even though she couldn't see me. I didn't know what else to say.

"So . . . looks like I won't be home till late. Will you tell Beech-man I'm sorry?"

"Um, yeah." I don't know what was wrong with my voice all of a sudden. I needed to swallow a bunch of times just to push the words through. "We'll just, you know, hang out here. We'll just be here. When you get home."

"I know you will. That's what keeps me going."

The line went quiet, and for a second I thought she'd hung up.

Finally she said, "You know you're the reason I'm doing this, don't you? You and Beech? I want you to have everything you need. Make sure Beech is always taken care of. And save for your college."

I swallowed again. "Don't worry about me. I can maybe get a scholarship. Like Rosalie."

"A scholarship." Her voice went quiet. "Yeah. A scholarship. That would help." She stopped. "A scholarship."

The line went quiet again.

"Mom?"

"I'll be home as soon as I can."

The phone clicked, and she was gone.

eight

I rustled *Episode Nine* open to the contest rules again and ran my finger down the crinkly page.

Judges' decisions final—check.

Prize nontransferable—check.

Entry postmarked by October 15—check. I circled the day on the calendar over my desk. I only had a few weeks.

I booted my computer and surfed to the Dark Overlord website. I clicked to the contest page, downloaded the entry form, and hit PRINT.

Because I, Tucker MacBean, was entering the Dark Overlord Sidekick Contest.

Or at least, my mother was.

Only she didn't know it.

And neither would anyone else. If my mother was going to win a scholarship, quit her cruddy job, and maybe spend a Sunday at home for once, nobody could ever know I was the true genius behind the prize-winning sidekick.

Not even my mother—until she absolutely had to. That was going to be tricky. One thing about my mom. She was a real stickler for following the rules, telling the truth, doing The Right Thing. All the stuff that makes you a better person and a respectable human being.

I rattled open my bottom desk drawer and pulled out a folder full of sketches.

I wasn't going into this thing unarmed. I'd been drawing comic books almost as long as I'd been reading them, and I'd created a whole gallery of superheroes. All I had to do was pick the best one and, with a few adjustments, turn him into the world's greatest sidekick.

I paged through my sketches.

First up: Ultraman. I set him aside. Too much like Superman.

Next: The Bulk. Nah. Too much like the Hulk.

LiquaMan. Too much like H2O.

Cosmic Cowboy. Too lame.

SweatSock Man. Too creepy.

See-Through Guy, composed entirely of plastic wrap. Too much . . . cold medication. (I was home sick from school the day I dreamed up *that* guy.)

Captain Hygiene. Please. Did I really draw that? How old was I?

I stared at the desk full of sketches. Maybe I *was* going in unarmed. What had happened to my superheroes?

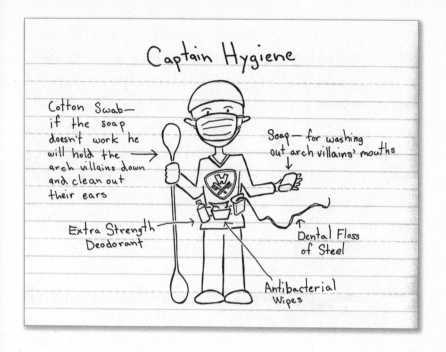

Captain Hygiene

Cotton Swab— if the soap doesn't work he will hold the → arch villains down and clean out their ears

Soap— for washing out arch villains' mouths

Extra Strength Deodorant

Dental Floss of Steel

Antibacterial Wipes

I remembered them being a lot more . . . super. And way more heroic.

See-Through Guy? Clinging to bad guys till they gave up in sheer annoyance? And Captain Hygiene? Wielding possibly the most feeble weapon in superhero history: Dental Floss of Steel. And no, the handy belt dispenser didn't ramp up the cool factor at all. What had I been thinking? This was worse than Sam Zawicki's lame fake superhero nickname: Beanboy. At least a bean could—

I stopped. A bean could do a lot of things, actually. Growing up with a last name like MacBean, I'd picked up more than your average amount of bean trivia, and I knew that beans were strong. Hardy. Full of protein. Bean plants enriched the soil and protected other plants.

61

And a single bean, if given enough water, could double in size overnight. In fifth grade science, we'd watched a germinating bean crack a rock in two. Not all at once, like an explosion. Gradually, over a few days' time. Which made me proud, given the affinity I feel for the bean. It proved that beans are both strong *and* relentless.

I tapped the end of my marker against my teeth. Watched the afternoon sun slide down the window of the Batcave.

Beans.

Strong and relentless.

Protector of others.

Works well with water.

I pulled a sheet of paper from my backpack and started to draw.

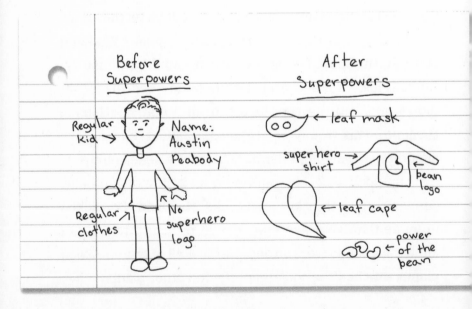

nine

I studied my Beanboy sketch. Snapped the cap off my marker and fixed a wobbly line on his mask. Even when I liked something I drew, I could always spot something I wish I'd done better. Like maybe Beanboy needed a better superhero hairdo. Something a little more super. And maybe less flat on one side.

Still, even with a flat head, Beanboy had turned out pretty well. He had a good cape. And a good logo on his stretchy crime-fighting shirt. In the superhero department, that was half the battle right there—the costume.

The other half was the coolness factor of his superpowers. I still hadn't figured that part out. But he already had a steadfast commitment to use his powers for good, which is pretty much mandatory in a superhero. And a strong chin. A superhero has to have a strong chin.

The afternoon sun had flung its final gasping rays against the Batcave window, and now the streetlight was my only protection against the graying night sky. As I drummed my marker against my desk, light from the streetlamp fell across the page, basking Beanboy in a sort of superhero glow. A glow that made him look fearless. Invincible.

But I knew Beanboy couldn't rely on streetlight glow. He had to be invincible without special lighting effects.

I opened *H2O, Episode Nine*. Ran my finger down the contest rules. Tore out the part that kept gnawing on my brain.

H2O's sidekick must possess the true heart of a hero. Reach deep within yourself, find that heroic heart, and create a sidekick who can rank among the greatest sidekicks in comic book history.

Find *my* heroic heart? Good luck.

I sighed. I'd have to fake it. I'd have to give Beanboy a heart so heroic, so fearless, no one would notice I didn't have a fearless heart myself.

I drummed my marker on my desk again. He'd need mind-boggling superpowers, of course. Excellent gadgets.

And a kick-butt origin story.

Because your major superheroes, the truly great ones, have great stories about how they got to be superheroes in the first place—stories that *give* them a heroic heart.

Take Bruce Wayne (a.k.a. Batman), devoting his life to avenging the murder of his parents. Or Marcus Poole (alias H2O), avenging the death of his faithful assistant, killed in a horrible lab accident. Or Peter Parker, struggling to balance normal life with the Spidey capabilities that brought him great power—and great responsibility. And also avenging the murder of his uncle.

I studied my drawing. "So. Beanboy. What's your story?"

"Beanboy?"

I jumped. Dropped my marker.

I'd been thinking so hard, I'd let my Spidey senses down. I didn't hear Beecher sneak up on me.

A good trick, considering Beech has zero sneaking powers.

He squinted at my drawing. "Superhero?"

"No. Not a superhero. Just a . . . guy."

"Not guy." He jabbed a little pointy finger at Beanboy's cape. "Superhero."

I blew out a long breath.

"Look. Beech. Beanboy is so super, so completely top secret, nobody can know about him. Okay? That means you can't tell anybody. *Anybody.* It'd be like—like if you went around telling people Superman was really Clark Kent."

He scrunched his face. "People know that."

"Well, yeah. People *here* know that. They've seen the movie. But not in Metropolis. What if you went around Metropolis telling everybody about Clark Kent? Then Superman couldn't save the world, because everyone would know his true identity. You don't want to ruin the world, do you?"

"I not ruin world."

"So you can't tell anyone about Beanboy."

"No. Tell. Anybody." He swiped his hands like an umpire calling a runner safe. "Ever."

Right.

I ordered a pizza and sent Beech to wait for the delivery guy. I pulled out a clean sheet of paper.

And was really zoning in. Till Beech:

1. Banged in with the pizza and thumped the door into my elbow.
2. Squeezed in to see my drawing. With his pizza-greased hands.
3. Jumped off the bed, clutching his slice of pizza, demonstrating superhero flight.

"BEECH!"

"I *sorry.*"

I looked at my ruined drawing. Then at my calendar.

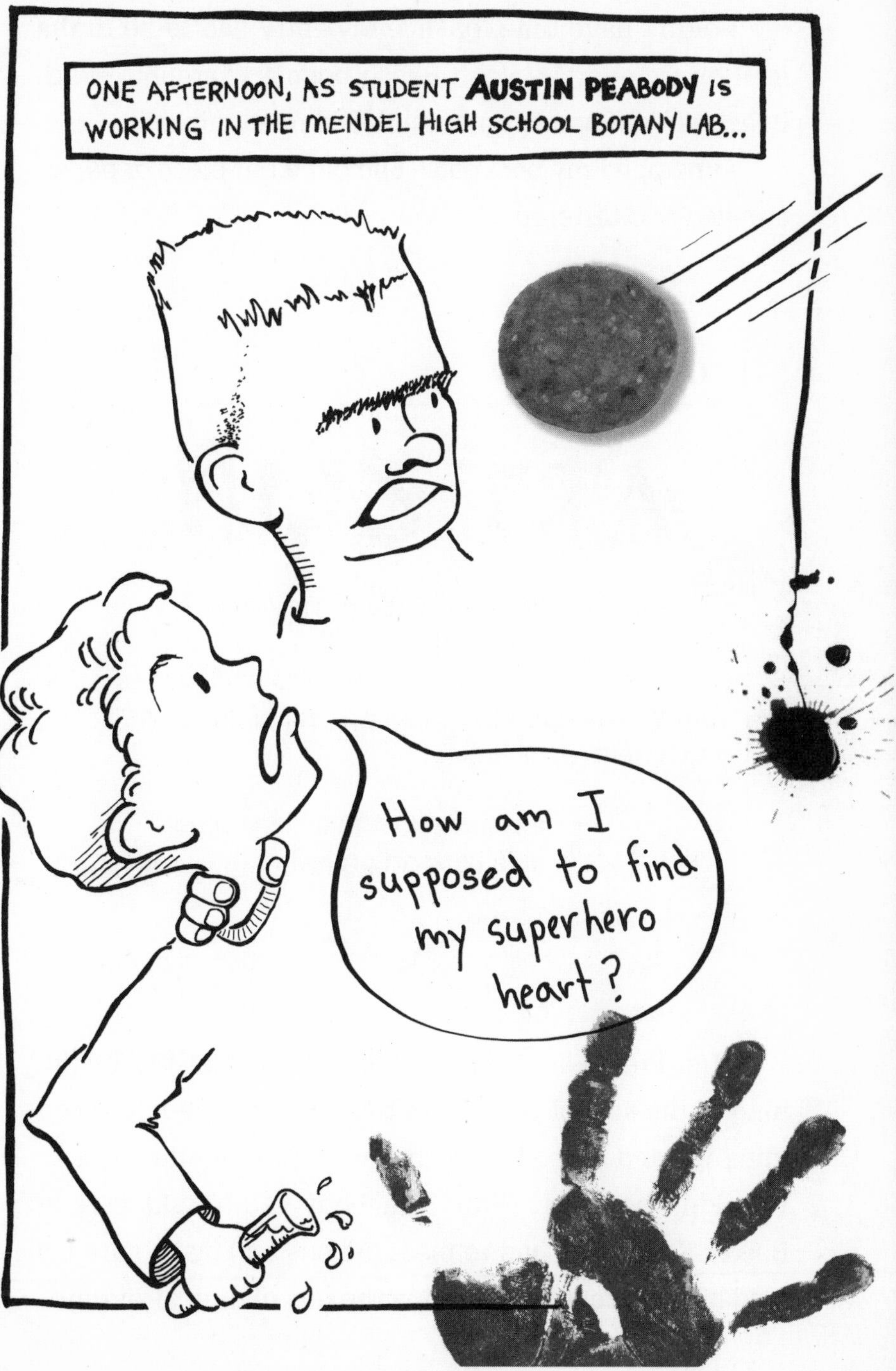
ONE AFTERNOON, AS STUDENT **AUSTIN PEABODY** IS WORKING IN THE MENDEL HIGH SCHOOL BOTANY LAB...
How am I supposed to find my superhero heart?

I didn't have time for this. My entry had to be in the mail by October 15. With Beech bouncing around—with Beech *always* bouncing around—I'd never make it.

I unzipped my backpack. Slid out a red piece of paper, crinkled and tattered.

JOIN

ART CLUB

Monday through Thursday
in the Art Room

Art Club members will enjoy a year of great art experiences, including:

- a chance to work on long-term individual art projects

Mrs. Frazee had passed the flyers out at the beginning of the school year. I don't know why I hadn't balled mine up and tossed it in the trash the minute I got it. I couldn't be in Art Club. Somebody had to take care of Beech. Somebody had to meet his bus and make sure his food had a face on it and wipe the goo off him afterward.

And there wasn't anybody left but me.

Still, for some reason, I'd slipped it into the pocket of my backpack, where I could take it out once in a while and make myself miserable knowing it was something I couldn't do.

Now I rubbed my finger over the crinkled last line: *long-term individual art projects.*

Translation: Drawing Beanboy *in the art room.*

I rustled through my desk and pulled out a pen and pad of stickies. I clicked the ballpoint.

Dear Rosalie,
If you don't have anything to do Monday through Thursday (starting tomorrow), could you babysit Beech while I do something after school? I'll pay you out of our pizza money. It could help with your pitiful scholarship budget.
            Tucker

When Beech went to the bathroom, I slipped out of our apartment and down the dark steps, hoping the MacBean Family Sticky Note System was powerful enough to include Rosalie. I pasted the note on the door of her festering sinkhole, then crept back up to the Batcave.

Step One of Tucker MacBean's Desperate Midnight Scheme: Complete.

Now for Step Two.

I smoothed the Art Club flyer on my desk. At the bottom was a permission slip. I clicked the ballpoint and—before I could talk sense into myself—signed my mother's name:

Mrs. MacBean

ten

To: BassoonMaster
From: SuperTuck
Subject: Right? Or wrong?

Noah,
If you do something wrong, it's wrong. Right? And if you
do something wrong for the wrong reason, it's like, double
wrong:

Wrong = Wrong
Wrong + Wrong Reason = 2 times Wrong

But what if you do something wrong for the right reason?
Does that make it only fifty percent wrong?

Wrong ÷ Right Reason = 1/2 Wrong?

If the wrong wasn't that bad and the reason was really, really right, it wouldn't even be half wrong. It might be like one-fourth wrong. Or one-sixteenth wrong. If something was only one-sixteenth wrong, it would barely be wrong at all.

Right?

Tucker

To: SuperTuck
From: BassoonMaster
RE: Right? Or wrong?

Um, Tuck? I don't think you can do math with right and wrong.

Just saying.

Noah

eleven

Late that night, way before my mom got home, I heard the entryway door creak open downstairs. Keys jingled. Footsteps tapped across the entry. I lay in my bed like a mummy—stiff, eyes closed, not daring to breathe.

Finally Rosalie's door scraped open, then shut again with a firm click.

I threw off my covers and stole downstairs through the dark, bare feet thrumming against the steps.

I found my sticky gone, another in its place. I peeled it off and held it up to the gray light.

Well.

That was that then. Tucker MacBean's Desperate Midnight Scheme, undone by a single sticky.

Tucker—

Sorry I can't watch the little guy. Quartet rehearsals are starting and I won't be home in time to meet his bus. Sorry

R.

I crumpled the note and trudged back upstairs.

And sat at the MacBean Family Kitchen Table, staring at my Art Club permission slip.

There had to be other babysitters.

I just didn't know any of them.

But my mom did. My mom knew practically everything. If there was a single person in Wheaton, Kansas, willing to watch Beecher MacBean after school, she would know that person's name.

Finally, I wrote another sticky.

I stuck it on the refrigerator.

Stared at it.

Peeled it off.

Stared at it some more.

Mom,
Is there any way I can
stay after school on
Monday through Thursday?
No big deal if I can't.
Love,
Tucker

Finally tossed it in the trash along with my permission slip. My mom didn't have time for this. I'd just have to work on Beanboy in the Batcave. And try to distract Beech with the cartoon channel.

I snapped off the kitchen light and started out of the room. The red permission slip caught my eye. A shaft of light from the streetlamp shone over the trash can, basking the paper in its own superhero glow. I pulled it out and flicked off a piece of leftover pepperoni. And almost tucked my sticky note back on the refrigerator.

But I didn't. I'd been right the first time. My mom already had too much to worry about.

I crumpled the paper into a ball and tossed it back into the trash.

It's almost like elves live in our house.

The next morning I stumbled into the kitchen, still rubbing sleep out of my eyes, and found a sticky on the fridge:

Tuck—
ART CLUB IS A VERY BIG DEAL. STAY AFTER SCHOOL. ROSALIE KNOWS SOMEONE TRUSTWORTHY TO WATCH BEECH. LOVE YOU. Miss You.

Mom ♡👄

P.S. YOU DON'T HAVE TO USE THE PIZZA MONEY.

If I'd known how to do a cartwheel, I would've done one right there in our kitchen.

twelve

How to Babysit Beecher MacBean

1. Get him off the bus.
   (this is the easy part)
2. Let him come upstairs by himself.
   (this will take some time)
   (if you make him hurry, it'll take longer)
3. Tell him to use the bathroom.
   (he won't go if you don't tell him)
   (trust me, you'll want to tell him)
4. Fix him something* to eat.
   (if he doesn't eat, he gets cranky)
   (you don't want him to get cranky)
   (*beige is your best bet)

I pasted the sticky on our refrigerator, next to the babysitting money Mom had left under a magnet.

thirteen

"So see?" My voice pinged off the lockers. I lowered it. "I *have* to join Art Club. I sure can't get any drawing done at *my* house."

We'd gotten to school early to turn my permission slip in, me and Noah. That time of morning, Earhart Middle was a lot less frantic than normal. The lights were softer. The halls bigger. The whole place smelled different. More like institutional pine-scented disinfectant and less like grubby pencil stubs and sweat.

Our sneakers squeaked along the freshly waxed floor tiles.

"Not with Beech around," I said.

First Rule of Lying: Include as much of the truth as you can. The real facts make the fake facts sound more true. Plus then you don't have to spend time making up every single thing. So I'd told Noah I wanted to create a comic book. And I told him about the pepperoni.

But I didn't say anything about Beanboy, and I sure didn't mention the contest.

Which made me a total traitor. A liar and a traitor. And, with the contest and everything, a cheat.

I couldn't suck Noah into my big old fat cheating lie. He'd never tell anybody on purpose, but what if he accidentally let it slip? Or, more likely, what if he tried to talk me out of it? I sure didn't need him giving me his disappointed look, like he'd always thought I was a better person than this, but now it turns out I'm not.

His face knotted in a frown. "But why now?"

Second Rule of Lying? Be prepared for questions.

"Well. See. I was sitting at my desk, and I slid open the drawer, and there he was, which was a big surprise since I'd pretty much forgotten about him, being as how I drew him way back in, I don't know, probably second grade, but you have to admit, in the comic book department I was pretty advanced, even in second grade, and once I saw him again, once I realized all that potential, just lying there in my desk drawer, well, I couldn't ignore it, could I?"

Third Rule of Lying? Once you start, it's hard to stop. It's like my mouth was a runaway train. It just kept thundering down the track.

Finally, to give my mouth a break, I held up my drawing of Captain Hygiene—exhibit A of my cover story.

Noah took the drawing. "Oh, hey. I remember him. So"—the frown knotted tighter—"this is your big hot project?"

"Yes," I said, trying not to be humiliated by the dental floss dispenser. "This is my big hot project."

Noah looked at me. Just looked at me. So hard I could practically see those brain cells beeping and blinking as they computed my truth quotient.

Fourth Rule of Lying: I suck at it.

"Okay," I said. "Here's the deal."

And I spilled my guts right there in the Amelia M. Earhart Middle School hallway. The contest. The scholarship. Everything.

I slid the Beanboy drawing out of my backpack and showed it to him.

Noah studied it.

"I know," I said. "I'm a disappointment as a human being. Tricking a scholarship out of a comic book company for my mom is wrong."

"Yeah." Noah looked up. "But an apartment without any parents seems more wrong."

He was still studying Beanboy. "Beans used as a power source." He nodded. "Plant life is sorely underrepresented in the comic book world. You could totally win."

He hiked up the bassoon case. I slid Beanboy back into my bag. We squeaked around the corner toward the art room—

—and almost ran smack into the shiniest girl in all of Wheaton.

Emma Quinn, all shimmery hair and glimmery teeth and glittery eyes, the fur on the hood of her sweater glistening across her back.

She was standing between the Kaleys—Kaley Timbrough and Kaley Crumm. They were taping orange sheets of paper to the walls and lockers. Kaley T. held the tape dispenser, Kaley C. slapped the paper against the wall, and Emma taped it at the top and bottom. Then they moved down the hall five feet and taped up another.

I lurched to a stop. Noah and the bassoon lurched into me. Just being in the same universe with Emma Quinn makes that kid flat-out clumsy.

Case File:
Emma
(She only needs one name. All you have to say is "Emma," and everyone at Earhart Middle knows who you're talking about.)

Status: Superhero
Base: Heaven, probably. I mean, that's probably what Noah thinks.
Superpower: The superhuman power to paralyze brain cells, even big brain cells like Noah's.
Superweapon: Blinding shininess
Real Name: Emma Quinn

Noah hiked up his bassoon case. "Hey, Emma."

She turned. "Hey, Noah." Her voice shimmered in the empty hallway. "Hey, Tuck."

"I-uh-uh-hey," I said. What was up with my throat?

Emma gave us her half-dimple smile. Her glance landed on Captain Hygiene, still clutched in my hand. She tipped her head to see better. Shiny hair bounced across her face.

"Oh." She nodded. "Superhero. That makes sense."

Now, most people saying that? It would come out mean. It'd come out: "Oh. Superhero. *That* makes sense." Translation: What *else* would a loser dweeb like Beanboy have under his armpit?

That's how it would come out if one of the Kaleys said it. All they did was look at us, the two Kaleys with their pink sweaters and their tape dispenser and their stack of colored papers. Just looked at us, then shot a sideways look at each other, a look that all by itself said, "Loser dweebs." Or, if we're being honest, more like, "Are you kidding me? How did we get stuck on the same planet as these loser dweebs?"

But coming from Emma—not mean.

See, me and Noah didn't always used to be just me and Noah. A long time ago it used to be me and Noah . . . and Emma. We all lived on Van Buren Street. Back when the tire swing was still a tire swing and not a flower pot. When we started kindergarten, our parents took turns driving us to school, and when we got there, we didn't know any better—we just piled out of the car and stuck together. Me and Noah and Emma.

That was before Emma's mind-jamming, brain-control superpower kicked in. Before anybody had ever heard of loser dweebs and hadn't yet figured out who would turn out to be one. Before first grade, when Emma moved to the other side of town. Way before my dad moved to Boston and we had to leave our house on Van Buren.

Emma handed one of the orange papers to Noah and another to me. The words FALL FLING marched across the top in big letters. Pictures of leaves floated down the edges.

"We're the planning committee for the dance. It's over a month away, but Ms. Flanigan put us in charge. It's the first time she's ever trusted seventh-graders with dance planning, and we can't let her down. We can't let the seventh grade down." She flashed a smile, beaming more shininess over us. "Are you guys going?"

The Kaleys rolled their eyes so hard I thought for a minute their eyeballs must've gotten wedged in the backs of their heads. They shot each other the look, which this time meant: "Are you kidding? It's not like anyone would dance with them, except maybe other loser dweebs, and how revolting is that?"

"I'm sure I will." Noah folded the flyer into a neat square and slid it into the pocket of his bassoon case.

"Dancing isn't my best talent, but I hate to miss a school activity."

"I—uh." I clutched my dance flyer. "Eeeergh." Man. This throat thing was getting worse. I was going to have to take some vitamins or something when I got home.

But my croak was drowned out by a *thunk, thunk, thunk.* At that moment, Sam Zawicki, of all people, rounded the corner, combat boots pounding against the floor tiles, straggly brown hair flying out from her head like flames, dilapidated backpack slung over her shoulder. She gripped a paper lunch sack tight in one fist. Glared at the orange dance flyers taped to the wall.

Kaley T. shielded the tape dispenser behind her back. Kaley C. clapped the stack of orange papers against her chest.

Sam thunked past. Or, actually, *through.* I was sticking out farther in the hall than Emma or the Kaleys. And it was like my power of invisibility had kicked in for real, because Sam plowed through me. Like I wasn't even there. Plowed her spear of an elbow into me so hard I'm pretty sure she punctured a lung. Her lunch sack got stuck on the strap of my backpack. The sack tore. A big round shiny red apple bounced out.

Sam stopped. Stared at the torn sack.

Narrowed her eyes. "What are you trying to do, Beanboy, *steal my lunch?*"

And you know what *I* said? After she mowed me over, impaled a vital organ, accused me of being a lunch thief?

84

I said, "Oh, uh, sorry."

Then I picked up her apple. Yeah. Picked it up, wiped the floor grit off on my jeans, and handed it back to her. That's what I did.

It was my mother's fault. My mother and all that politeness she'd been drilling into my young, impressionable head my whole life. Good manners kicked in before I could stop them.

Sam snapped her head back. Snatched her apple from my hand.

And suddenly noticed Emma and the Kaleys and their stack of flyers, watching her. Her face boiled deep red.

And even though I can barely admit this, even to myself, well, I kind of understood the whole boiled red thing.

I've been that color. You know, when you're just wandering along minding your own business and suddenly look up and find the whole world looking back at you?

What I didn't get, what I never got about Sam Zawicki, was what she did next.

She pierced Emma and the Kaleys with a glare, a glare that—seriously—should have drawn blood. Then she smiled, the Zawicki Smile of Death, turned, and marched back down the hallway, dragging her hand along the wall, ripping the dance flyers loose, leaving a flock of colored papers fluttering behind her.

The Kaleys shrieked.

Emma's mouth dropped open.

They scrambled to retrieve the crumpled flyers. Noah scrambled to help.

I started to scramble. But mainly I just stood there. Staring after Sam. Thinking how, no matter what happened, she always managed to make it worse for everyone, including herself. *Especially* herself. Because who wants to hang out with somebody who drowns comic books or rips up dance flyers? Why would somebody go around *trying* to make people hate them?

So there I was, standing in the middle of the hallway, trying to figure out Sam Zawicki, of all people. Which is how I happened to see what she did next.

She ripped the last flyer off the wall, but instead of letting it flit to the ground, she jammed it down into her combat boot.

That creeped me out, and not because she was steal-ing a flyer. What creeped me out was, she stuck it in her boot. Don't get me wrong—the shoe really is the best place to store valuables, no matter what Noah says.

It just creeped me out that Sam Zawicki had figured that out too.

fourteen

I hunkered over the scarred desk. Around me, seats squeaked, papers rustled, rain thrummed against the window behind Coach Wilder's desk.

I barely noticed. I shielded my health notebook with one arm and scribbled furiously, black marker gliding

Calcium - Good for teeth and bones
Vitamin A - Good for eyes
Thiamine - Deficiency causes beriberi (whatever that is. I'll ask Noah later. Now that he's taking 7th grade health, his parents have probably signed him up for a beriberi study group).

across the page. Coach Wilder was no doubt impressed by my sudden enthusiasm for the digestive system. By the sheer volume of notes I seemed to be taking.

And I *was* paying attention. Mostly. And jotting down stuff that might pop up on a test.

But mainly I was drawing. I had to.

When I'd handed my permission slip to Mrs. Frazee that morning, she'd tucked it into her grade book and said Art Club was for art lovers of all stripes, even those who came late to the table. Whatever that meant. But she also said she'd see me at Art Club after school.

Now it was seventh hour, the last hour of the day, and I was creating Beanboy's arsenal of superpowers. When I stepped into Art Club that afternoon, I needed to be ready to draw.

I sketched Beanboy sprouting to giant proportions:

Beanboy, muscles bulked by the Power of the Bean, bold and unflinching in the face of Madame Fury's freeze beam:

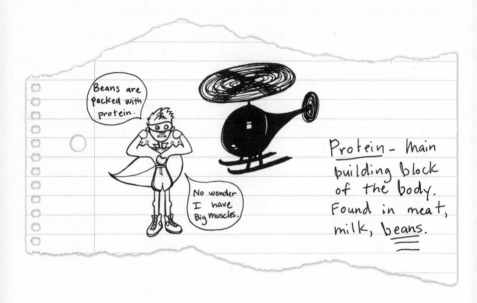

Beanboy wielding indestructible bean tendrils as skillfully as Spidey wielded his web . . .

. . . cinching the tendril tight as he hovered—

My marker scritched to a stop. Hovered? Could Beanboy hover? I studied my drawing. So far, his superpowers—superhuman agility, unbreakable tendril lassos, instant elevation from his sprouting beanstalk legs, the ability to produce massive amounts of oxygen from carbon dioxide in a flash (allowing him to survive underwater, a big bonus in the H2O universe)—all flowed from the Power of the Bean.

Beans couldn't make you fly.

Could they?

I studied my drawing. Beanboy would make a way better sidekick if he possessed some kind of aerial skill. Even though oxygen would come in handy, and a decent lasso was pretty much a superhero necessity, so far Beanboy possessed lame-o superpowers. Plus he had to battle Madame Fury and her Helicopter of Doom.

I tapped the end of the marker against my teeth. Stared into space.

And I realized I was staring *at* something. Or, actually, some*one*—Sam Zawicki.

I snapped my gaze away. Making eye contact with Sam Zawicki never turned out well. Look what happened with *H2O* and the mud puddle. And the dance flyers.

And the humiliating third grade bathroom incident.

Okay, here's what happened: We were all lined up in the hallway after lunch, waiting to use the bathroom. And

I noticed my shoe was untied. So I bent down, and while I was busy tying, the line moved forward. When I stood up and turned to say something to Noah, I found myself nose to nose—

—with Sam Zawicki.

I whipped back around so fast that as my mother would say, I let a windy.

Or, as Noah said, his eyes all big: "Wow. You really ripped one."

Or, as the whole third grade chanted, while my windy echoed through the hall: "Beans, beans, the musical fruit, the more you eat 'em, the more you—"

I stopped. Stared at my Beanboy drawing.

It was the most famous fact about beans, the one thing everyone, even if they'd never heard another single bean factoid in their lives, knew by heart: The more you eat 'em, the more you . . . toot.

Tooting, a.k.a. passing gas, a.k.a. cutting one, was not normally considered a virtue. But that's only because nobody had ever harnessed its power for good.

It's universally acknowledged that there are different categories of, well, farts: the loud, embarrassing kind that honestly don't smell that much, and the quiet killers, silent but deadly.

The first could power Beanboy's flight:

And the second could be the ultimate superhero weapon:

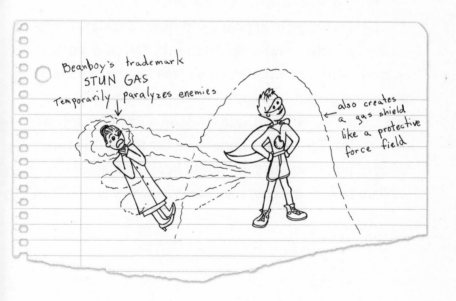

I hunched over my notebook and drew, dizzy with creativity—or maybe marker fumes—amazed that nobody had thought to elevate farting to a superpower before.

It's surprising how cheerful excess gas could make me. Noah sat two seats over. I caught his eye and flashed him a thumbs-up. His face knotted in a confused frown. I'd have to bring him up to speed on Beanboy's skills after class. If anyone could appreciate the transformation of an awkward bodily function into a superpower, it was my friend Noah Spooner.

I was so cheerful, before I even knew what I was doing, I glanced over at Sam Zawicki.

Again.

My eyes were clearly out of control.

She was sitting in her desk, furiously scribbling notes.

Except she wasn't scribbling in her notebook. I squinted. She was scribbling on a small yellow square of paper. She peeled it loose, opened her binder, and carefully lined it up on the inside cover, in a row of other yellow squares. She ran her finger over the top to make sure it stayed put, then carefully closed her binder again.

Sam Zawicki had her own sticky note system.

fifteen

The bell rang and I darted upstream, a salmon swimming against the current of middle schoolers fleeing for the exits. I made it to the art room and settled into my desk in the far corner.

Other Art Club members wandered in in clumps, laughing and talking, and pulled out their projects. Art activity buzzed around me.

Mrs. Frazee made a couple Art Club announcements (mainly involving the dangers of dumping clay down the sink). Then she caught sight of me.

"Let's get you started," she said.

She dragged me across the room, propped her glasses on the end of her nose, and began shuffling through the art books on the shelves behind her desk. Her face, tanned and wrinkled, puckered as she read through the titles. Her loopy turquoise earrings swayed beneath her wild red hair. One by one, she pulled out a mountain of books, all about drawing comics.

She loaded them in my arms, then led me to the art supply closet, unlatched the lock, and threw open the door.

And at that moment I swear angels started to sing. A golden light burst from within the closet, and I felt the very breath rush out of me. I almost dropped my stack of books.

Because for a comic book artist like me, this was a closet of wonder: shelf after shelf of bottles and tubes, brushes, pens, pencils and erasers, stacks and heaps and mountains of paper, lined up in rows and neatly labeled.

"Bristol board can get expensive, so I don't bring it out for everyday projects. But for something like this, it would be much better than our usual drawing paper. Much harder surface." She thumped her finger against a stack of thick white paper. Her bracelets jangled. "Gives you nice crisp lines."

I stared at her. Bristol board? She was letting me use real Bristol board?

I had no idea what Bristol board was, but it had to be better than what I'd *been* using: computer paper swiped from my mother's printer. Plus my health notebook. And pizza toppings.

Mrs. Frazee balanced several sheets of the board

on top of my stack of books and tucked a black drawing marker behind my ear.

"There." She gave a nod. "That should get you started."

"Thanks," I said.

I crunched across the art room floor, gritty from old ceramics projects. Other Art Club members were bent over their desks. Pencils scritched against paper. Paintbrushes clanked against water jars. A grubby radio with a bent antenna blared a tinny tune from a shelf in the corner.

To me, it sounded like the angels were still singing.

I unloaded my pile on my desk, then climbed onto my stool, took a deep breath of turpentine-flavored art-room air, and squared a sheet of Bristol board on the tilty desktop in front of me. I ran my hand across the board. Mrs. Frazee was right. It was smooth and shiny, perfect for a superhero.

I was almost afraid to draw on it. I didn't want to mess it up.

But I also couldn't wait to get started.

I pulled the marker out from behind my ear. Hunkered down behind my stack of books. Snapped the lid off the marker.

And started to draw.

And suddenly, it was like I was in the zone. I don't think I'd ever been in the zone before, so I couldn't be positive, but it sure felt like the zone, with my marker gliding across the Bristol board, all these great sidekick ideas gliding across my brain cells, and music from the bent-antenna radio gliding into my ears.

I kind of hated to jinx myself by thinking about it, but the future of the Tucker MacBean universe was— suddenly, and for the first time in a really long time— looking bright.

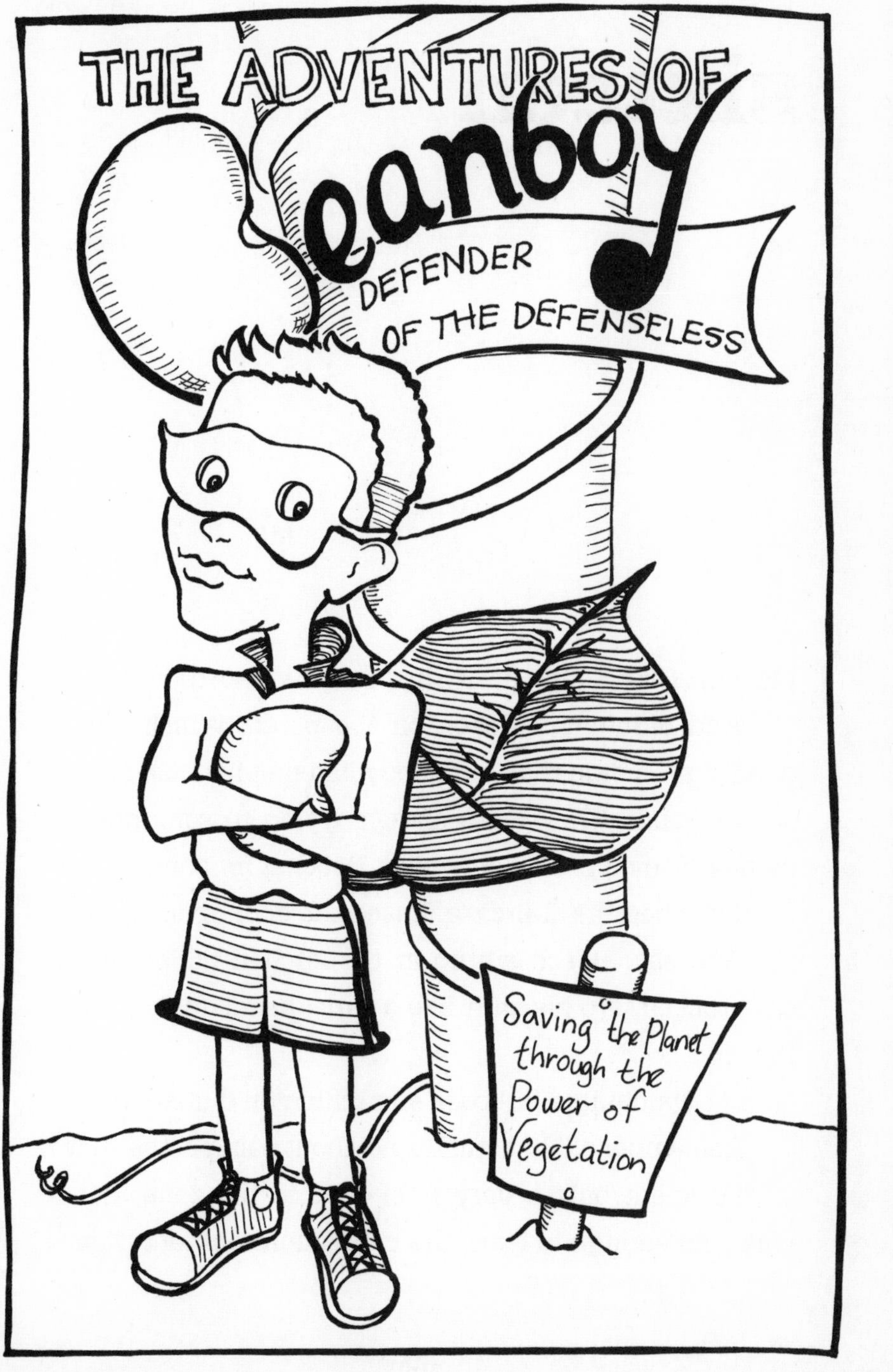
THE ADVENTURES OF
Beanboy
DEFENDER OF THE DEFENSELESS
Saving the Planet through the Power of Vegetation

sixteen

I left Art Club a little early. Just in case. Raced home.

And didn't find Beech on the porch. Which was a good sign. A sign that somebody had met his bus. Maybe Joe or Samir. They were always trying to scrounge up money. They'd probably babysit Beecher for some cash.

I climbed the staircase. Eased the door open.

And saw Beech sitting at the kitchen table, pillowcase tucked into his shirt like a cape, hands folded in his lap . . .

. . . watching a girl cook something on our stove.

Remember all that stuff I said about being in the zone?

I'd spent only a very brief time in the zone, but it was long enough to learn the most important fact: Zones aren't permanent. Zones have no loyalty. Zones will lull you into thinking that the world is finally spinning in the right direction, that the universe is finally on your side, and then they'll turn around and smack you in the head without warning.

The girl wore combat boots and an army surplus jacket. Her straggly brown hair flew out from her head like flames.

She scraped something out of the skillet with a spatula and flipped it onto a paper plate.

It was a grilled cheese sandwich. A slightly crooked grilled cheese sandwich, a little burnt on one side, with raisins fried right into the bread and potato chips tucked into the top corners for ears.

"Face!" Beech looked up at her, eyes wide with admiration. "You made happy face!"

Sam Zawicki glanced up. Caught me watching her from the doorway.

"Close your mouth, Beanboy. You look like a guppy."

Beech pointed a stubby finger at me. "You a guppy." He giggled. "Sam funny."

Yeah. Hilarious.

"So." I closed the door behind me. "You're, um . . . babysitting."

Maybe not the most genius thing I'd ever said.

Sam narrowed her eyes. The spatula quivered in her white-knuckled fist.

And honestly? Standing there in the glare of the overhead kitchen light, with the sink dripping and the radiator rattling and Sam Zawicki shooting death rays from her eyeballs, all I could think was: Why? Why was she always so mad? All I did was walk into my own house. Quietly. And found . . . her.

If you ask me, *I* should be the one who was mad.

So many things were just so completely wrong about this.

"About time you showed up." Sam's bark shot across the kitchen, raspy and harsh, like she'd gotten a piece of sandpaper wedged in her throat.

"I—what?" I looked at her. "I'm not even late." I flung a hand toward the clock on the microwave. "I'm early."

"Yeah. And that's not going to happen again." She jammed her hand into her jeans pocket. Fished out a wad of yellow paper. Uncrumpled it and slapped it on the table—*bam, bam.*

"Notes!" Beech ran a finger over the wrinkled yellow squares, then looked up at Sam, admiration beaming from every subatomic particle of his face. "We note, too."

He pointed at the fridge, at the sticky note I'd stuck there this morning, next to the babysitting money.

I snatched the note from the refrigerator. Everyone had a bathroom, I guess. But the whole world didn't need a visual aid of our hygiene issues. Plus I'd drawn a heart at the bottom.

"See?" Beech grabbed my wrist and held it up. The

Mom,
We're out of toilet paper.
Beech went a little
crazy.

♡ Love,
Tucker

P.S. The toilet's clogged.

little corners of yellow paper poked through my clamped fingers. "Note!"

Sam looked at him, and the death rays dimmed a little. Her teeth unclenched. Her wood-grinder voice spun down to low. For just that second, her elbows didn't even look all that pointy.

But just for that second, and then she was all spikes and sandpaper again.

"Here's the deal, Beanboy." The teeth re-clenched. "If I'm going to keep helping you—"

Help? Did she seriously think—

"Wait." I stopped. "*Keep* helping? You mean . . ." — I blinked— "you're coming back?"

"Yeah. I'm coming back." The death rays gunned me

down. "I promised your mother. What do you think, I'm irresponsible or something?"

Well . . . *yeah*.

She jabbed a finger at the first sticky, then crossed her bony arms over her chest.

I squinted at her handwriting, smaller even than Noah's, neat and precise, like little soldiers marching across the sticky note:

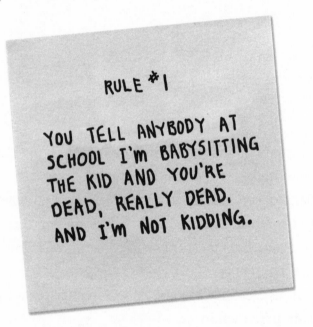

Tell anybody at school? Was she crazy? In a thousand million wadzillion light years I would never tell anyone Sam Zawicki had been in my house. Not even Noah.

Not even *me*. That was true. I would wipe the data from my brain and never think of it again. That's how much I would never tell a single soul that Sam Zawicki had been here babysitting Beech.

"No problem," I said.

"No problem," said Beech.

"And you can't tell anybody, either," I said. Just so she'd know she wasn't the one in charge around here.

She rolled her eyes. Jabbed the second note.

RULE #2

5:00 MEANS 5:00, SO DON'T BE LATE, AND DON'T BE EARLY AND TRY TO KEEP SOME OF MY MONEY FOR YOUR OWN BONY-BUTT SELF.

Bony-butt? Sam Zawicki was calling *me* bony-butt?

And plus, we'd had plenty of babysitters before, mostly Rosalie, and not once did I ever keep any of her money.

Also, this was my house. Sam Zawicki couldn't boss me around in my own house. On a sticky note.

She pushed away from the counter, snatched the babysitting money from under the refrigerator magnet, and stalked out of our apartment, muttering something that sounded like: "I unclogged your toilet." The door banged shut behind her.

I stood there for a second watching it quiver from the impact.

"You tare her."

I looked at Beech. "Tear her?"

"No. *Tare* her." He gave me a hard look. Trying to drill the information into my brain with his eyebrows, I guess. Then, in pure exasperation, he gnarled his fingers into monster claws, bared his teeth, and let out a "Rahhhrrrr!"

I blinked. "Scare her?"

He dropped his monster claws to his sides.

"I promise you, Beech-man, there is no way I could scare Sam Zawicki."

He looked at me.

"Nobody can. She's unscareable." I pushed his glasses up.

He shook his head and picked up his grilled cheese sandwich. He started to take a bite, but one of the potato chips fell off. He studied the one-eared happy face for a minute, then set the sandwich back on the plate, climbed down from the table, and trudged from the kitchen.

"'Tare her," he muttered as he clomped down the hall to his room.

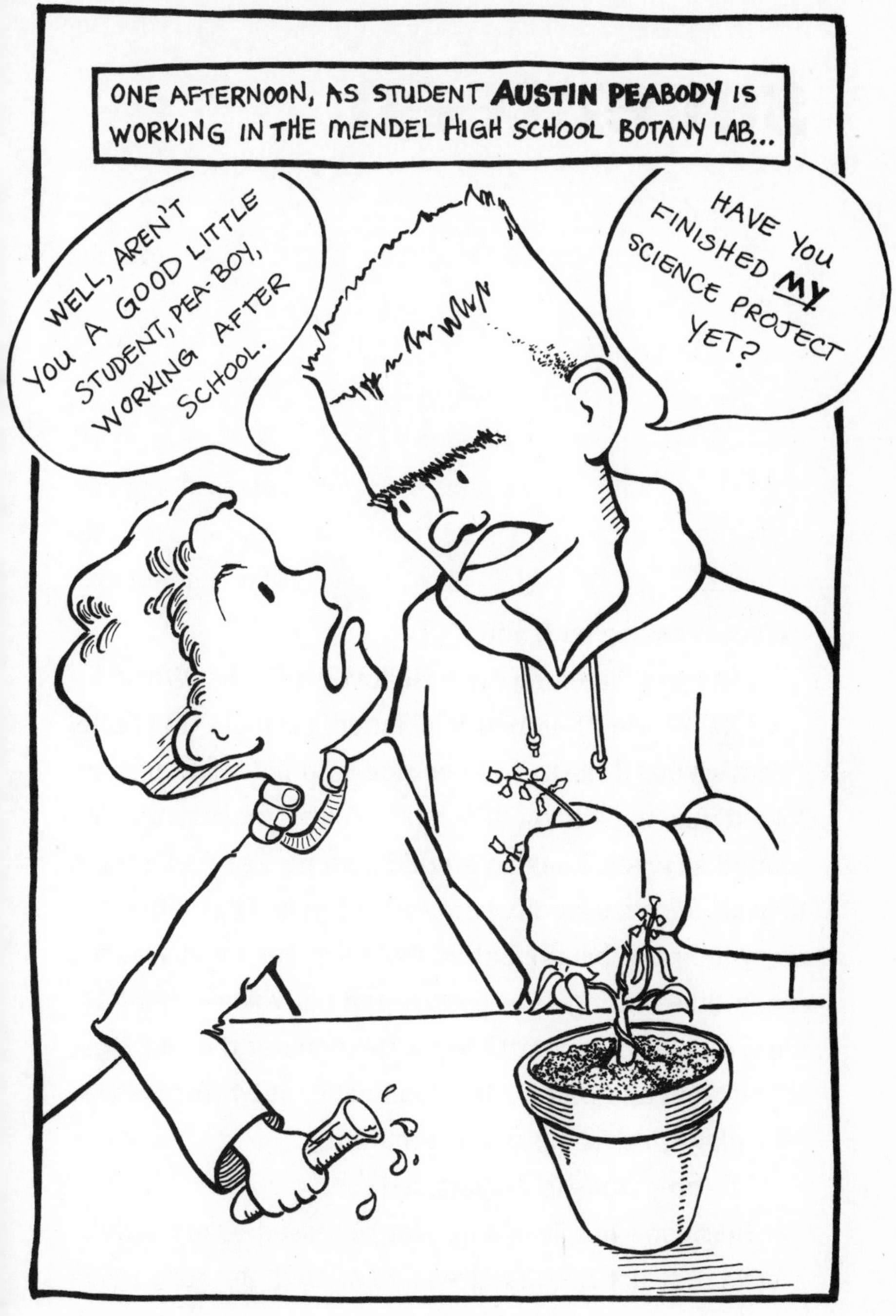
ONE AFTERNOON, AS STUDENT **AUSTIN PEABODY** IS WORKING IN THE MENDEL HIGH SCHOOL BOTANY LAB...
WELL, AREN'T YOU A GOOD LITTLE STUDENT, PEA-BOY, WORKING AFTER SCHOOL.
HAVE YOU FINISHED MY SCIENCE PROJECT YET?

seventeen

"What is wrong with you?"

I jumped. Snapped my gaze toward Noah. "What?"

"See?" He thumped his lunch tray on the table. "That's what I mean." He settled into his chair and unfolded his napkin on his lap. "You've been sneaking around all week. Peeking around corners. I say something to you, and you about jump out of your skin. Plus, I'm sorry to bring this up, but you've been spending way too much time staring at"—he lowered his voice—"her." He cut a quick look toward the far table under the EXIT sign, where Sam and Dillon Zawicki always sat by themselves. "It's like you're obsessed or something."

"I—ob—wha—?" I sputtered.

Because—no. Just—no. Not obsessed. Okay, maybe a little. But not because I was *obsessed*. Because I was creeped out. You would be too. So would Noah. Because Sam Zawicki had been at my house, she was coming back—often—and there was nothing I could do about it.

I had to go to Art Club. I had to. And Sam Zawicki was my best option.

Noah was still looking at me.

"Okay," I said. "Maybe I glanced at her. Once. Or twice. But only for research." I picked up my fork. Stabbed at my chicken and noodles. "For, you know, possible arch villains."

He kept looking at me.

"I'm serious," I said. "If you were creating a villain, who would you use for research?"

"Sam Zawicki."

"Okay then." I shoveled the noodle into my mouth and started to chew.

Fifth Rule of Lying: Anyone can do it if they're desperate enough.

■ ■ ■

When I walked into the art room that afternoon, Mrs. Frazee reached into the depths of the art supply closet and pulled out a crisp new pencil with light blue lead.

"It's non-repro blue." Mrs. Frazee handed it to me. "You'll like it."

Wow. A non-repro blue pencil. I ran my thumb over the tip. I *did* like it. I had no idea what it was, but I liked it.

I liked it even better once Mrs. Frazee explained how it worked.

"You do your sketch with the blue pencil, then ink your drawing right over the sketch. You don't have to erase the sketch lines because the printer won't pick up this particular color of blue. Non-repro means it doesn't reproduce. It should save you some time and aggravation."

I settled into my tilt-top desk in the corner and started drawing.

And I had to admit, Beanboy was coming along. Having the Power of the Bean was like having a jet pack, only better because it was built in. Kind of made you wonder how other superheroes attained flight.

I sketched out the comic book panels with my blue pencil.

Take Superman. Everyone thought he had some kind of born-in-another-solar-system thing going on. But what if he didn't? What if the planet Krypton had nothing to do with it?

I started inking over the blue pencil lines.

What if he was secretly using the whole musical fruit system, too, and was just too embarrassed to admit it?

Beanboy wasn't embarrassed. Beanboy was tooting to save mankind.

Still, I couldn't help wondering if the Power of the Bean gave my comic book what it needed to win the contest.

As cool as it was, excess gas just might not be enough.

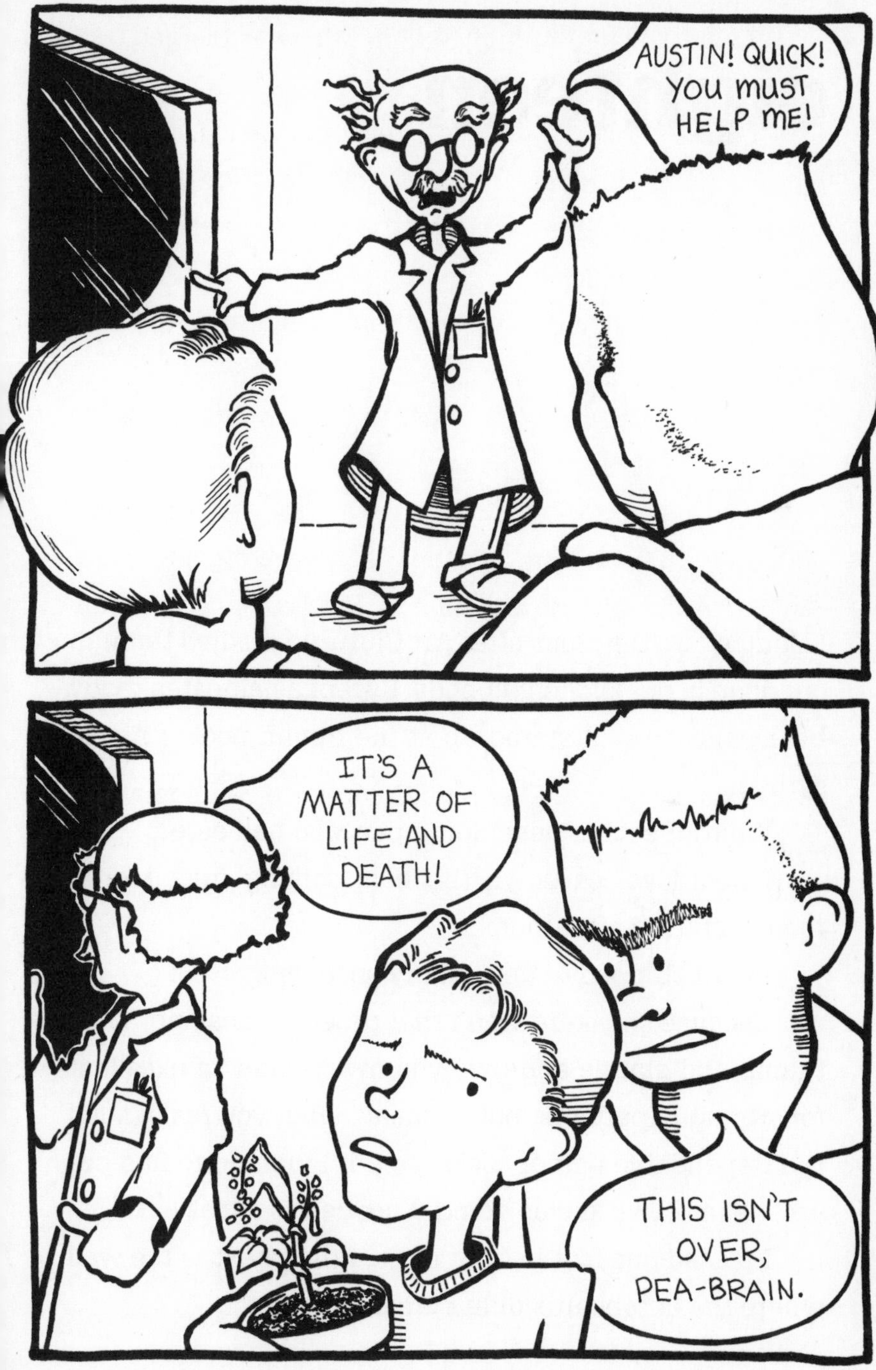
AUSTIN! QUICK! YOU MUST HELP ME!
IT'S A MATTER OF LIFE AND DEATH!
THIS ISN'T OVER, PEA-BRAIN.

eighteen

I clomped up the steps after Art Club and pushed through our door. In our kitchen: nobody. Except a half-eaten teddy bear pancake that stared up at me from a pool of maple syrup.

Weird. Beecher never left a pancake half eaten.

I heard voices down the hall, coming from Mom's room. I started after them.

First I stopped to take off my sneakers.

Because sneakers aren't that great at sneaking. They thump and shuffle and give you away. They're excellent for storing paperwork, but to sneak, what you really need is a dependable pair of socks. And if I wanted to find out what Sam Zawicki was doing, I needed to sneak.

I placed one foot in front of the other, next to the wall where the floorboards didn't creak.

"You tool, Sam." Beecher's voice floated out from Mom's room. "You rot."

"You showed me this stuff, kid." Sam's bark floated out, too, most of its sharp edges filed down. "You're the one who rocks."

"No. You rot, Sam. Really."

"Not as much as you."

Oh, brother. Hard to stay quiet when you're trying not to hurl the Skittles you chowed during Art Club.

I reached Mom's door, inched my head around the door jamb, and pretended I was part of the woodwork.

This was just weird. I mean, Superman doesn't go all Man of Steel while relaxing in the Fortress of Solitude. Batman doesn't throw the Batarangs when he's hanging in the Batcave with Alfred. But here I was, calling up my Power of Invisibility in the MacBean Family Apartment.

Sam was sitting on my mom's rug, her back toward me. Beech sprawled beside her on his stomach, chin resting on his hands, watching whatever fascinating thing she was doing.

Which looked like writing. Or no—drawing.

My mom had this giant sewing box Grandma had given her. She only ever used it to make Halloween costumes or mend something Beech had ripped, but it was filled with all kinds of stuff—thread and needles and pins and buttons and this weird thing that looked like a pizza cutter for really tiny pizzas, plus all these old patterns in their crispy, yellowed envelopes.

Now it was in the middle of the floor, with the lid hanging open. Dusty patterns lay in a circle around Sam. She picked one up, squinted at the picture, picked up another, then hunched over to erase something on her drawing.

Erased and erased. And erased. And I could have told her what was going to happen: She erased a hole right through the paper.

"Unh!" She tossed her pencil. "I don't know why I thought I could do this."

Beech elbow-crawled under Mom's desk and retrieved the pencil. He crawled back and handed it to her. "Tut draw, too. He really good."

"I know." Sam crumpled her drawing into a ball. "He draws his little stupidheroes all over everything."

Now that was just insulting. Because no, I didn't. Not on everything. Just the Bristol board from Mrs. Frazee. And my health notebook. And sometimes, in an emergency, a napkin during lunch. And once, accidentally, the cover of my algebra book, but I erased it.

And not only that, superheroes weren't stupid. Well, maybe Captain Hygiene.

"Not stupid." Beech gave Sam his one-eyed, scrunched-nose thing. "Super." He looked at her hard so that she'd understand the difference.

And right about now, you're probably thinking, *Hey, that invisibility thing comes in handy. You find out stuff you wouldn't know any other way.*

Like, at that very moment, I found out that even

though Beecher's brain had been sucked into the Zawicki Mind-Warp of Unbelievable Weirdness, when pushed to the wall, he was still Beech. He'd still make a stand for his brother and for the one thing we both believed in: the superness of the superhero. Kind of made my heart thump, in a good way.

Then the dark downside of invisibility smacked me in the face: *You find out stuff you wouldn't know any other way.*

Because Beech was still looking at Sam, nose scrunched, trying to make her see the difference between stupid and super, counting off superheroes on his fingers. "Spidey super. Batman super. Eight-two-oh super. See? Super."

And Sam, all prickly with her hard elbows and clenched shoulders, looked down at him—and did the weirdest thing.

She smiled.

Like she didn't want to, and tried not to, but couldn't help it. He did look pretty goofy, all scrunched up and serious like that.

Still. What was wrong with her? With everyone else in the known universe, Sam Zawicki was this evil alien life form bent on destruction. With Beech, she was almost a . . . person. Like maybe she *hadn't* been hatched from a shriveled gray space pod. At least, not a hundred percent.

She pushed Beecher's glasses up. Her eyebrows smoothed out. I swear even her hair unstraggled a little.

I could've lived my whole life without seeing that.

Beech unwadded Sam's drawing and tried to smooth it out on the rug.

Sam pulled it away from him. "Don't worry about it, kid. It's almost five o'clock anyway." She tossed it into Mom's trash can under the desk. "Let's get this stuff picked up."

■ ■ ■

After Sam had snatched her babysitting money from my hand and stomped out, and Beech had gone back to eating his cold, dead pancake, I crept back to Mom's room.

I pulled the drawing from the trash and smoothed it out. Turned it one way, and then another. Until I figured out what it was supposed to be: a dress. Or maybe a bathrobe. No, I was pretty sure it was a dress. There were straps involved, and I'm no expert, but I'd never seen a bathrobe with straps.

I stared at it, wondering why the heck Sam Zawicki wanted to draw a dress.

And don't ask me why. Maybe because Beech said I was good at art. Maybe because I knew what it felt like to try to see something all perfect in your head and then watch it come out all wrong on the paper. Because maybe I'd erased holes in my drawings before.

Or maybe because I lost my mind for five minutes. That's probably it.

I studied Sam's drawing. There wasn't much to go on, especially with the hole right there where the armpit should've been. But I started to get an idea of what she was trying to do. I dug through the sewing box till I found the patterns she'd been squinting at. It looked like she'd taken pieces and parts of different patterns and stuck them all together in one dress. I spread the patterns out and drew the dress again on a clean sheet of paper.

And it turned out pretty good. A real dress somebody might actually wear. I even threw in some sparkles—a comic book artist trick—which gave it kind of a movie star look.

Not that suddenly I was a fashion designer or anything. But sometimes superheroes turn out to be girls, and sometimes they have to dress up and go undercover or something (they can't wear a cape *all* the time), and a comic book artist needs to know how to draw their clothes. And sometimes those clothes need to be sparkly. That's just a fact.

Still. Probably wasn't a great idea to let anybody see it, at least not till I got famous.

I stuffed the drawing and the patterns into the sewing box and shoved it back under Mom's desk where it belonged.

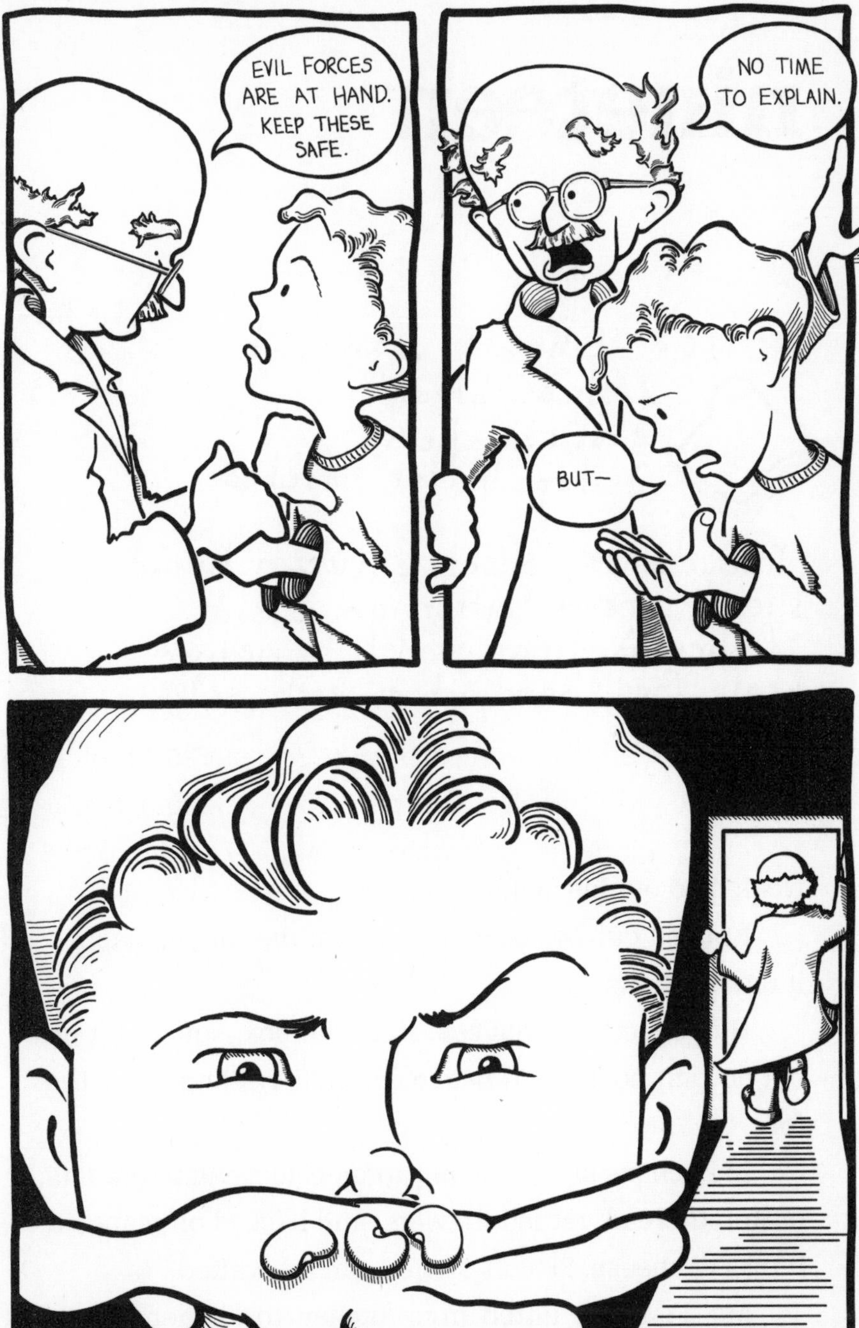
EVIL FORCES ARE AT HAND. KEEP THESE SAFE.
NO TIME TO EXPLAIN.
BUT—

nineteen

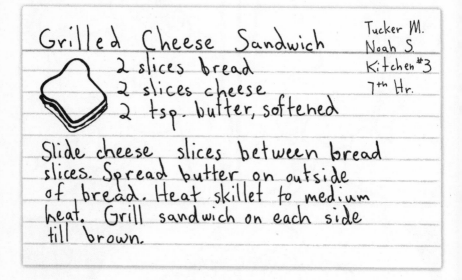

Grilled Cheese Sandwich
      2 slices bread
      2 slices cheese
      2 tsp. butter, softened

Tucker M.
Noah S.
Kitchen #3
7th Hr.

Slide cheese slices between bread slices. Spread butter on outside of bread. Heat skillet to medium heat. Grill sandwich on each side till brown.

Noah held out his hand. "Cheese."

I pulled our box of Velveeta from the fridge. Slapped it into his hand.

He slipped the Velveeta from the box, squared it on our cutting board, and began carefully peeling away the foil.

In kitchens all around us, apron-clad seventh-graders buttered bread, rattled drawers, and hacked off mangled hunks of cheese. Skillets sizzled. Smoke wafted.

Ms. Flanigan flitted from kitchen to kitchen, chef's

hat bobbing on her head, staving off potential culinary disasters. You wouldn't think much could go wrong with a grilled cheese sandwich and canned soup. But we were seventh-graders. Seventh-graders with stoves. Ms. Flanigan was understandably nervous.

Stoves. I stopped. A bean wouldn't want to be cooked. Would it? Could that be his weak spot, the chink in his armor, his kryptonite?

Uh, no. That was just pathetic.

"Tucker." Noah's voice was a sharp hiss. "I don't need to remind you that Ms. Flanigan wields the toughest grade book in Earhart Middle. If she comes over"— he cut a glance toward Kitchen #4, where Ms. Flanigan was scratching something in her home-ec-teacher grade book—"and sees we haven't even buttered our bread, we're going to lose some serious Time Management points." He held out his hand. "Cheese slicer."

I rummaged through the drawer, pulled out the slicer, and slapped it in his hand. He steadied the Velveeta and began carving slices with the precision of a surgeon.

"Look at them." He lifted his chin toward Kitchen #1, Emma's kitchen, where Kaley T. was ripping the foil off their Velveeta in little chunks. "At this point I'd say we definitely have the lead in the Food Prep points department."

Uh-huh. And at any point I'd say Noah was a little too competitive in the grade point average department.

I cut another glance at Kitchen #1. Kaley C. was wrestling with their gallon of milk. She finally got it opened and—

"Oh, man," I said.

—dropped the whole thing in their sink. Milk glugged into their dishwater. Dirty soap bubbles seeped into the milk jug.

"That's going to lose them some Ingredient Handling points," said Noah.

No kidding. Poor Emma. With the Kaleys in her kitchen, her grade didn't stand a chance.

By this time, Noah had covered our cutting board with cheese slices, lined up like flat little soldiers. We buttered and assembled our sandwiches. As we set them in the skillet to cook, Ms. Flanigan's voice cut through the FACS room.

"Fresh food, seventh-graders. Remember, it's all about fresh food prepared in a healthful and flavorful . . ." Her voice trailed off. "Dillon, dear, I believe that knife is a little large."

The Zawickis were also in seventh hour Food and Consumer Science, in Kitchen #6, right across from us. The Zawickis, meaning Sam, of course, plus her brother Dillon, who was actually an eighth-grader (but way bigger than anyone else in the eighth grade, including the teachers and most of the coaching staff), who flunked seventh-grade FACS last year and had to take it over and was relying on his sister to help him pass.

I glanced up. Dillon Zawicki had dumped their Velveeta onto their cutting board and was now circling it, trying to figure out an angle of attack. Armed with a very large butcher knife.

Ms. Flanigan fluttered over. "We don't want to mutilate our cheese, do we?"

Dillon considered this. He didn't seem convinced that mutilated cheese was a bad thing.

Ms. Flanigan turned to the class. "Remember, seventh-graders, you'll enjoy more success in the kitchen if you choose your utensils wisely. It's not always about using the largest and, uh"—she stole a glance at the butcher knife—"sharpest tool. It's about using the right tool for the job."

She slid open a drawer.

While Sam and Dillon watched Ms. Flanigan, Kaley C. reached over and slid the Zawicki milk jug from their counter. She flipped the lid off and began measuring out milk for their soup.

Nobody saw her. Except me. And for a second I did a little inside-my-head cheer for Kaley C., of all people. At least now Emma wouldn't lose points for Improper Recipe Procedure.

Kaley recapped the milk and was about to slip it back into the Zawicki kitchen when Ms. Flanigan whirled around. Kaley thumped the milk back down onto her own counter.

"I think you'll find this a little easier to use." Ms. Flanigan set a cheese slicer on the Zawicki cutting board and removed the butcher knife from Dillon's hand. "We won't be needing this, will we?"

She balanced the knife on her grade book and paused to scribble a few notes.

Sam watched her. "Are you taking off points?" Her voice was actually kind of quiet for once. Not the usual bark that slapped you into the next county.

"I have to, dear." Ms. Flanigan finished scribbling and dotted something with a big flourish. "We've had several class discussions about appropriate tool use. Dillon's judgment was a little shaky this time, but if you two work hard for the rest of class, you should be able to salvage the project."

Ms. Flanigan frowned at Dillon, who was now taking their bread in for a layup against the refrigerator door.

She tsked her tongue. "Do I need to call your mother?"

Dillon stopped. "My mother?" He tucked the bread under his arm. "That'd be great. If you get a hold of her, tell her I want to talk to her, too. It's been a while."

Sam froze.

Ms. Flanigan stared at the two of them, then scribbled something else in her book. She straightened her chef's hat and flitted off to avert a scorched skillet disaster in Kitchen #1.

Sam watched her go. Closed her eyes, her mouth set in a grim line.

She opened her eyes—

—and caught me watching her. And for a split second she looked . . . embarrassed. Okay, maybe just surprised. Or probably not even that. This was Sam Zawicki we were talking about. Sam Zawicki, who'd never been surprised by anything in her life. It was probably just a trick of the light or something.

It only lasted a split second anyway, and then she was back to her usual: the Zawicki Glare of Death.

"What are *you* looking at, Beanboy? You think this is funny?"

"No. I wasn't—"

"Just cook your stupid sandwich and leave us alone."

Yeah. Like I ever wanted anything to do with Sam—or any Zawicki—in the first place.

"Oh, no." Noah's voice was a strangled groan.

I glanced over—

—and saw smoke curling up from our skillet. While we'd been watching Ms. Flanigan, the edges of our grilled cheese sandwiches had sizzled to a crispy black.

Noah closed his eyes, his face knotted in anguish and despair. "I can't believe I let myself get distracted like that. I'm acing advanced Spanish, advanced English, and ninth grade chemistry. I can't flunk grilled cheese sandwiches. How would that look on my permanent record?"

I glanced up. Ms. Flanigan was overseeing a boiled-over soup disaster in Kitchen #4.

"She hasn't noticed," I said.

"She will. She can sense burnt from fifty paces. She'll

take off points in every category—Time Management, Equipment Maintenance, Ingredient Handling, Recipe Compliance. She'll make up whole new categories just so she can take off points. We're doomed."

I stared at the burnt crusts. No way could I stay after school to redo the whole project. No way could I miss Art Club.

I slid our utensil drawer open and burrowed for what we needed. "I give you"—I held up a large metal cookie cutter—"extra credit."

Noah eyed the cutter. His anguish and despair began to melt.

Because the one thing Ms. Flanigan loved more than anything, the one thing sure to make her give out extra credit points, was Food Presentation, or, as she put it, "arranging your meals in the most attractive and appealing manner possible." According to Ms. Flanigan, good presentation could trick your brain into thinking the food tasted better than it actually did. She'd looked up a bunch of scientific studies that said so.

If anybody knew how to trick somebody into eating, it was yours truly, Tucker MacBean. It was probably my best talent. It was the one skill I possessed that came marginally close to a superpower.

It was the only thing keeping my brother alive.

And now it was going to save our sandwiches.

Noah scrubbed the black stuff off our skillet before Ms. Flanigan's Spidey senses could kick in. I wielded our cookie cutter with skill and precision and buried the burnt-crust evidence in the trash. We fanned our sandwiches across a plate and stood back to admire our masterpiece.

"Gingerbread men!" Ms. Flanigan and her chef's hat bobbed to our kitchen. "Or should I say, grilled-cheese men." She held our plate up so seventh hour could see it. "Class, this is what I mean by food presentation."

She set the plate down and bobbed off, scribbling stars in her grade book as she went.

Noah punched my arm. "Dude," he whispered. "You saved us."

Yep.

I did.

Me and my cookie cutter.

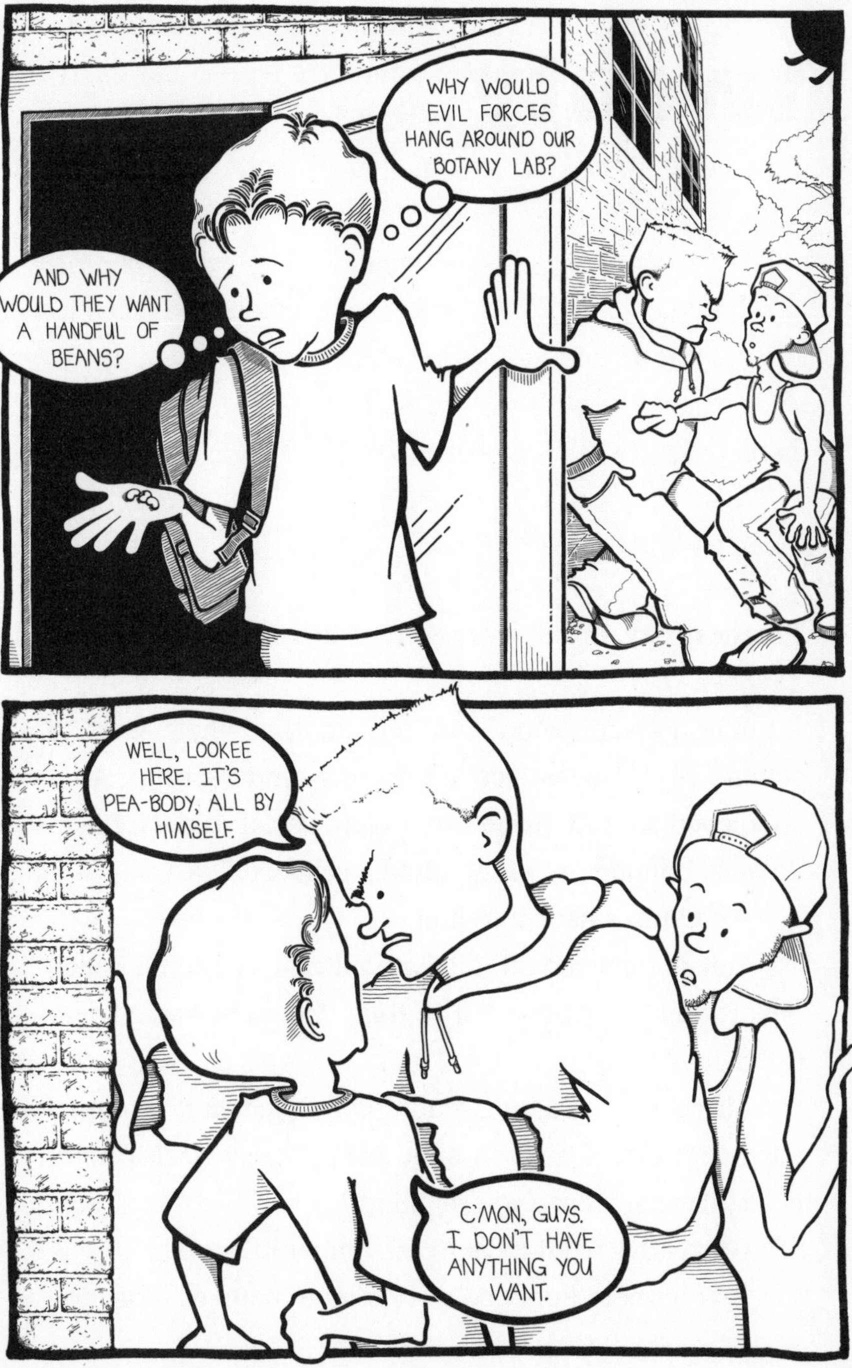
WHY WOULD EVIL FORCES HANG AROUND OUR BOTANY LAB?
AND WHY WOULD THEY WANT A HANDFUL OF BEANS?
WELL, LOOKEE HERE. IT'S PEA-BODY, ALL BY HIMSELF.
C'MON, GUYS. I DON'T HAVE ANYTHING YOU WANT.

twenty

The next day, on my way to first hour, I ran into Dillon Zawicki.

It'd been blowing and raining the whole way to school, and I was soaked to my undershorts. As I squelched around the corner toward social studies, Dillon Zawicki banged out of the middle school office.

And I ran smack into him.

Sort of bounced off. Like a gnat bouncing off a beach ball. Dropped my books, of course. They skittered all over the hallway.

"Hey. You." Dillon's mud-crusted sneakers clomped past. Left a size sixteen shoe print on my health notebook. "Watch where you're going."

Good advice. I'd have to remember it.

As I gathered my books, two more pairs of shoes followed Dillon out of the office. I looked up. One pair, neat and polished, belonged to Mr. Petrucelli, who was wearing his serious principal face and smoothing his serious principal tie. The other, a pair of work boots, belonged to an older guy, thin, compact, his face as brown and worn as his boots. Wisps of white hair twanged out at odd angles on his head, like they were surprised to be there.

It was the guy from the farmers' market. The guy with the wagon.

I stared at his work boots. Muddy. Battered. Soaked through from the rain. Held together with duct tape.

I blinked. I'd seen those boots before. And not just at the farmers' market.

I'd seen them on Quincy Street. This was the same guy who'd been carrying the ratty paper bag out of the thrift store. The bag of something fluffy and pink. The day Sam Zawicki drowned my comic book. I'd been a little distracted at the time, so I'd almost forgotten.

But I'd seen those boots clomping down the street outside Caveman.

Mr. Petrucelli looked down. "Tucker." He raised a serious principal eyebrow at me. "Don't you have somewhere else to be?"

Somewhere besides the shoe grit and broken pencil lead in the middle-school hallway?

"Yes," I said. "Yes, I do."

I tucked my books under my arm and skirted around Dillon.

The work boot guy thrust his square, leathered hand toward Mr. Petrucelli. Mr. Petrucelli gripped it and they shook, the muscles in the man's ropy arms standing out tan and work-worn next to Mr. Petrucelli's crisp white principal shirt.

"I'm sure sorry you had to take time out of your day to call me down here," the man said. "I apologize for all the fuss my boy caused."

My . . . boy?

I stopped. Looked at the guy. Then caught Mr. Petrucelli's serious principal frown, and started walking again.

That's when I noticed Sam. She'd been there the whole time, I guess, but I sure hadn't seen her, and I don't think anybody else did, either.

She was pressed into a corner, between a locker and the door to the math room. She stood very still, holding her binder tight to her chest, watching over the top of it. Almost as if she was trying to be . . . invisible.

■ ■ ■

I brushed Dillon's footprint off my health notebook and squared it on the table next to my lunch tray. Stared at the empty page, trying, once more, to think how I was going to lift Beanboy up to the ranks of the major comic book sidekicks. Like Robin. Or Jimmy Olsen. The truly great ones.

I needed something powerful. Like a villain. Yeah. A powerful villain could bring out the superhero heart of a sidekick. I stared at the blank page.

But my brain cells kept drifting to something else.

My boy.

That's what the work boot man had said: *My boy.*

My boy, meaning . . . Dillon?

I cut a quick glance at the table under the EXIT sign. Where Sam was sitting. Alone. Rain hammered the windows behind her.

According to the Earhart Middle School Information Hotline (a.k.a. the Kaleys and their friends and everybody who listened to them, which was, well, everybody), Dillon had been suspended for a week.

I picked up my spoon. "Do you think that guy was Dillon Zawicki's father?"

Noah shrugged. "Anything's possible."

"But he looked too old. And way too small. I mean, he was regular size, but you know Dillon. He's a baby T-rex."

"So maybe it wasn't his father." Noah wiped his fork and spoon with his napkin, then spread the napkin neatly on his lap. "Maybe he was somebody not even related."

I frowned. Dragged my spoon through my pudding. "Like who?"

"Like, knowing Dillon, possibly his probation officer."

Probation officer. I licked pudding from my spoon.

"That makes a lot more sense," I said. "Except, I don't

really see a probation officer holding his boots together with duct tape, do you?"

"How would I know?" Noah held his hands up. "And what difference does it make?"

Well, none. Probably.

Still, the whole thing seemed weird. Everybody had to come from somewhere, but I never thought of Dillon Zawicki having an actual . . . family. Except for Sam, of course, but that didn't prove much.

Lightning split the sky beyond the lunchroom windows.

Lightning. *That* was powerful.

I picked up my pencil.

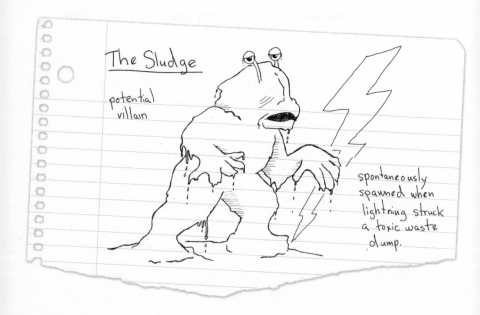

The Sludge

potential
villain

spontaneously
spawned when
lightning struck
a toxic waste
dump.

Noah studied the drawing over my shoulder. "Not bad."

I nodded. The Sludge *wasn't* bad. He'd make a pretty good bad guy.

Assistant bad guy, anyway. A henchman to the true arch villain.

I sighed. A pretty good henchman wasn't good enough. A pretty good henchman had never brought out the superhero heart in anyone.

I tapped my pencil against the drawing.

Glanced at the table under the EXIT sign again. At Sam, who sat with her head down, chewing a bite of peanut butter and jelly, just about glaring a bullet hole into her lunch sack.

She was Sam Zawicki and everything, so she probably didn't even care, since she hated pretty much everyone, but sitting by yourself at lunch had to stink. I mean, Dillon wasn't much in the lunch buddy department.

But now she didn't have *anybody*.

■ ■ ■

Sam didn't say a word to me when I got home from Art Club.

I was pretty much used to that. It worked out well for both of us, since I didn't want to talk to her, either.

But for some reason, today her silence seemed more,

135

well, silent. She didn't bang around the kitchen so much. The Zawicki Glare of Death seemed more like a smolder than a laser blast. And when she left, she didn't slam the door hard enough to rattle it off the hinges.

Even Beech seemed quiet.

After she was gone, he shook his head. "Sam sad." He wandered off to his room, his pillowcase cape drooped over his shoulders, muttering something that sounded like, "No tune-up. No money. No dress."

Who even knew what he was talking about?

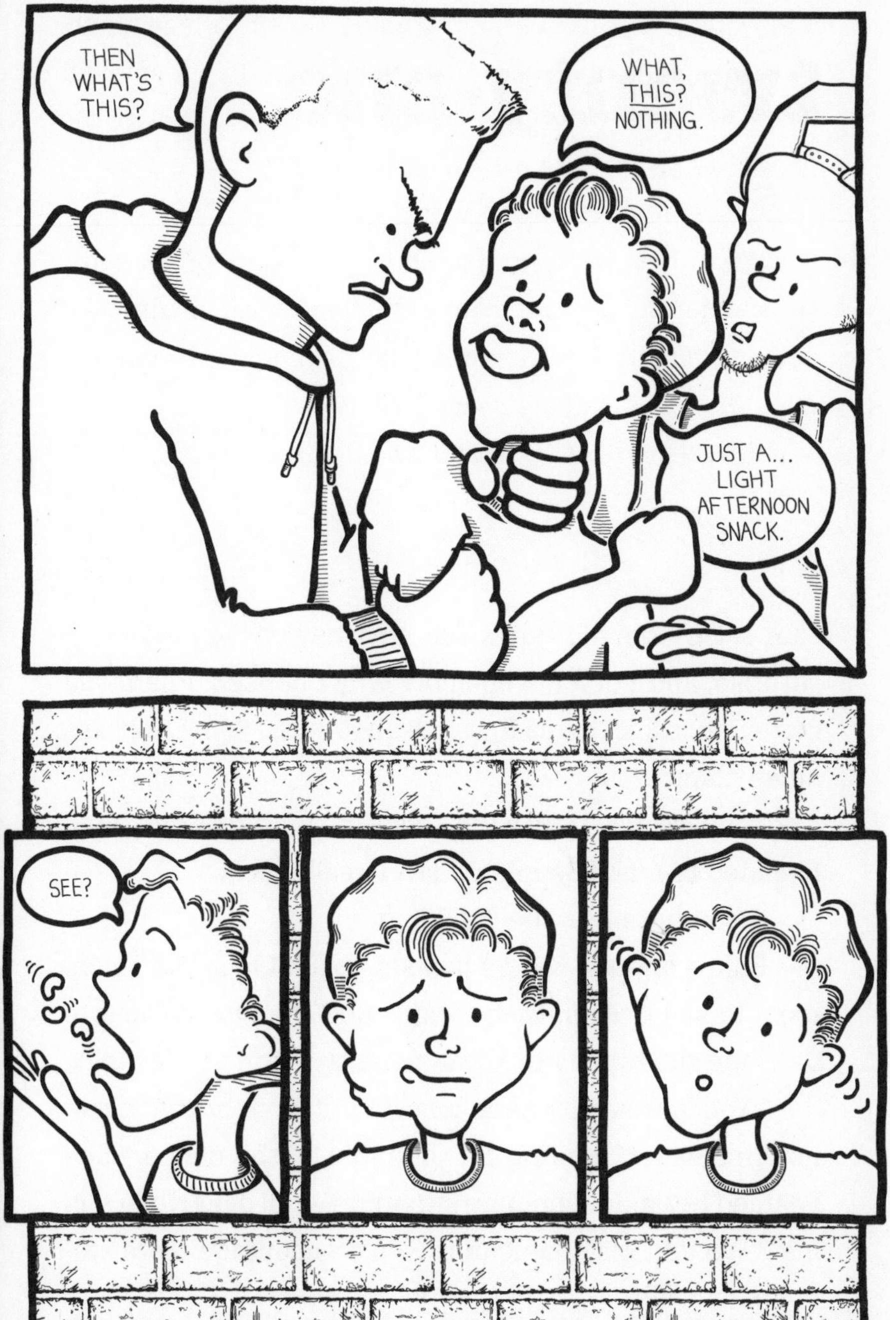
THEN WHAT'S THIS?
WHAT, THIS? NOTHING.
JUST A... LIGHT AFTERNOON SNACK.
SEE?

twenty-one

Sam sat by herself again the next day. Which wasn't a surprise, and I don't even know why I noticed. I had way more important things to worry about than Sam Zawicki's lunch plans.

For instance, I still hadn't come up with that one thing I needed to make Beanboy's story really rock.

Also, there was the Fall Fling.

Emma and the Kaleys had set up a table in the lunchroom to sell tickets. Emma explained the whole thing to us while she taped her ADVANCE TICKETS sign to the table.

"You get a fifty-cent discount if you buy a ticket now instead of waiting for the night of the dance." She beamed her mind-jamming superpower all over Noah and me. "We told Ms. Flanigan it would encourage more students to come."

"Good idea," Noah told her.

"Urr-guh-yeah," I said.

So Noah and I got in line to buy tickets. Because even though the Kaleys were probably very possibly right, and nobody would dance with us, we couldn't let Emma down, not after she went to all the effort of setting up a table and making a sign and everything.

The line inched along. I jingled my money in my pocket, not paying attention to who else might be in line in front of us.

Until the Kaleys, who always had *something* to say, went dead quiet. And a barky voice growled out a single word: "One."

I snapped to attention. It was Sam. Zawicki. She stood three people ahead of us, at the front of the line. From the looks of it, she was trying to light Kaley T.'s hair on fire with a Zawicki Glare of Pain and Dismemberment.

Kaley T. stared at her. "One . . . ticket? To the . . . *dance?*"

"Yeah. To the dance. What else would I be standing in this stupid line for?"

The Kaleys shot each other a look. A sideways loser dweeb look.

Kaley T. turned back to Sam. Gave her a sweet, concerned, and completely fake smile. Pulled a ticket from her pile and acted like she was going to hand it to Sam, then pulled it back.

"Are you *sure* this is the best use of your money?" she

said. "I mean, if your family can't even afford *milk* . . ." Her voice trailed off. She raised an eyebrow.

Milk? I looked at Kaley T. Then at Kaley C., who suddenly, for some reason, decided at that very minute to count her stack of tickets.

"What did you say?" Sam's growl was quiet, but even from the back, I knew her face was burning red. She clenched her fists. Her hair crackled with rage.

Kaley T. sighed a completely fake concerned sigh. "Don't get mad. I'm only worried that—"

"Kaley." Emma's voice was sharp. "We're here to sell tickets." She snatched the ticket from Kaley T.'s hand and held it out to Sam.

Who stood there for a really long moment, fists still clenched.

"Forget it," she said finally. "I wouldn't come to your stupid dance if you paid me."

She whirled, shot the entire line down with a machine-gun glare, then stomped across the cafeteria, her combat boots practically shattering the floor tiles, and clanked out the door.

For a second, the whole lunchroom went silent.

Then it erupted in conversation, everyone talking at once.

Kaley T. rolled her eyes. "She makes such a scene out of *everything*."

Emma looked at her.

Kaley C. looked at her pile of tickets.

The line inched forward.

"Well, it's *true*," Kaley T. said. "Her *brother*"—she wrinkled her nose, like she'd just gotten a whiff of something rotten—"stole a whole gallon of milk from the FACS room."

"Milk?" I said.

Noah glanced at me. I closed my mouth.

"She can't help what her brother does," said Emma.

Boy, *that* was true. I'd spent my whole life trying to help whatever Beech did, and I'd never made a dent. And Beech was way smaller than Dillon.

"Besides," said Emma, "we don't even know for sure he did it."

"Yes, we do," said Kaley T. "Why do you think he got suspended? They can't kick somebody out just for being a big, stupid jerk. Although, really, I don't know why not. When Ms. Flanigan checked their kitchen, their entire gallon of milk was just"—she threw her hands in the air dramatically (you could tell she liked telling this story)—"gone. And then, when she asked him about it, he lied—to her *face*—and said he didn't take it. That's why he got suspended. For stealing and lying. And not only that, his family has to pay for the missing milk."

Kaley C. studied the flaky green polish on her fingernails.

"They paid for the milk? But"—I stared at the Kaleys—"what about the other kitchens? Was everybody else's milk there? Like, say, yours?"

Kaley C. didn't move.

Kaley T.'s nostrils flared. "Of course it was. We don't steal." She picked up her stack of tickets, clearly finished with the conversation. "So are you going to buy a ticket or what?"

I stuck my hand in my pocket. Fingered my dollar bill and four quarters. It was plenty for my Fall Fling ticket. With two quarters left over.

"Um, Noah?" I whispered. "Can I borrow a dollar from your emergency bassoon case fund? I'll pay you back. I just . . . didn't bring enough."

Kaley T. rolled her eyes.

Noah shrugged. "Sure."

He swung his bassoon case around, unzipped his emergency supplies pocket, pulled out a dollar, and handed it to me.

I doubt he would've been so casual if he knew what I was planning to do with it.

I let Noah go ahead of me. He bought his ticket and shuffled off to the side to zip the bassoon case.

I slid the two dollars and four quarters across the table to Emma and held up two fingers.

She flashed her half-dimple smile. "Oh, you need—"

She stopped. Got this really thoughtful look on her face and glanced at the cafeteria door, which was still vibrating from Sam slamming through it. She beamed her smile on me again, only this time it was full dimple.

She slipped my money into the metal cash box and

handed me two tickets, tucked together so that no one could tell she was holding more than one. "You're a good person, Tucker MacBean."

"Ar—guh—yigh," I said. Which, roughly translated, meant *No, I'm actually a really stupid person, but thank you. Let's hope I live through this.*

I tucked both tickets in my shoe and shuffled across the cafeteria after Noah.

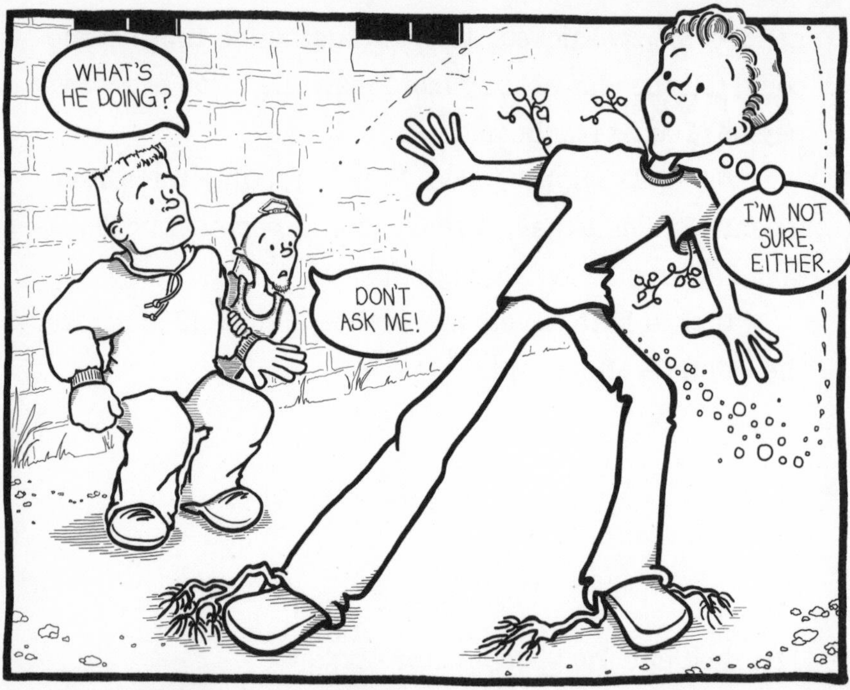
WHAT'S HE DOING?
DON'T ASK ME!
I'M NOT SURE, EITHER.

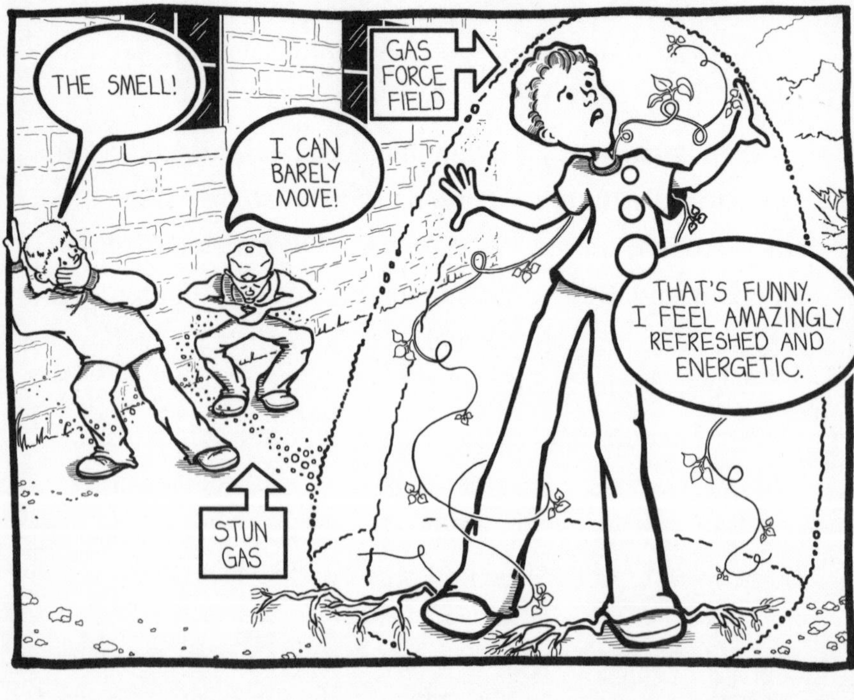
THE SMELL!
I CAN BARELY MOVE!
GAS FORCE FIELD
STUN GAS
THAT'S FUNNY. I FEEL AMAZINGLY REFRESHED AND ENERGETIC.

twenty-two

I trekked into the kitchen after Art Club.

Beech was sitting at the kitchen table, wearing the pillowcase and eating macaroni with a cut-up hot dog face.

Sam was doing . . . something, I guess. I didn't look at her. I usually didn't. We'd gotten into a pretty good routine. I didn't look at her. She didn't look at me. I didn't say anything. She didn't say anything back. She babysat Beech. I handed over the babysitting money. She left.

Worked out pretty well for everybody.

So I marched straight to the refrigerator, as usual. Slid the money from under the magnet and covertly folded it in half. It was a little bulkier than usual, but I hoped nobody would notice. I turned and handed the whole wad to Sam.

She snatched it from my hand, heaved her backpack from the chair, said "Bye, kid," as she ruffled Beecher's hair, and banged out the door. Beech and I listened to her boots thump down the stairs.

The thumps stopped, and for a minute, all we heard was silence.

Beech looked at me. I closed my eyes. I'd been hoping she wouldn't find it till she got home.

The footsteps thumped back upstairs. The kitchen door flew open.

Sam stood in the doorway, holding the Fall Fling ticket in the air like a machete.

"What is this?"

I swallowed. "Looks like a dance ticket."

She mowed me down with a glare. "I *know* that. What was it doing in my babysitting money?"

"Um . . . because I put it there?"

Sam narrowed her eyes. "Quit being stupid on purpose. You know what I mean."

I closed my eyes again. Why did she have to make everything so . . . hard? Why couldn't somebody just do some tiny little thing for her that was just a tiny bit nice without having to run for cover?

I took a breath. "Look," I said. "It's not that big a deal. It's just that, well, the Kaleys are mean to everybody. They're mean to me, too. But mostly they just give me the loser dweeb look and leave me alone."

"Loser dweeb look." Sam stopped breathing fire long enough to consider this. She nodded. "Yeah. That's about the right name for it."

Beech nodded, too. "Right name for it."

As if he even knew what he was talking about. He just wanted to be like Sam, which was too scary for me to think about right then.

"They're not going to waste the full impact of their superior meanness on a lightweight like me," I said. "So they shoot the loser dweeb look, remind me I shouldn't be allowed to breathe the same air as them, and that's it. They don't actually, you know, *say* anything to me."

Sam snorted. "Lucky."

Beech snorted, too.

By this time Sam had relaxed a little. She was still holding the ticket, but more like a piece of paper than like a weapon. Even her hair had smoothed down so it wasn't in full-attack position.

And I should've stopped right there.

But me, being *me*, I had to explain things further.

"So since I was standing there in line anyway," I said, "I figured I could buy an extra ticket without being totally run out of the cafeteria—"

The very second those words left my mouth, I knew they were wrong.

"*What* did you say?" Sam's hair snapped to full alert. "You think the Kaleys *ran* me out of the cafeteria?"

"No. I just—"

"For your information, I left on my own. Because I wanted to. Not because anyone ran me out."

"I know. I didn't mean—"

"No one runs me out of anywhere, you got that?" She pointed the ticket at me. "I know how people look at me. I know they think, oh, she's just one of those scroungy Zawickis, can't even buy her clothes in a normal store. Like I'd really *want* to dress like everybody else and go to some lame dance and be like those stupid Kaleys, who can't even decide what to wear without texting each other first. But they did not run me out of the lunchroom. You got that?"

She stopped to catch her breath, her bony chest heaving with rage, the ticket shaking in her white-knuckled fist.

"And just so you know, even though you probably don't care, my brother is not a thief. He's sure as heck not sneaky enough to get a whole gallon of milk out of the FACS room without anybody noticing. He does a lot of stupid things, and I spend a lot of time trying to undo them because my grandpa has enough to worry about—"

"Wait." I blinked. "Your grandpa? So . . . the man with the white hair. He's not your father?"

"My father? Are you kidding me?" Sam sputtered, her face so red, I thought her head would pop right off her neck. "I've never even *met* my father. We're not as lucky as you, Beanboy. We don't have a mom or a dad just hanging around the house waiting to stick pizza money on our refrigerator. But we pay our own way. We pay for our own milk, and we pay for our own dance tickets, so you can keep this."

She flung the mangled ticket on the table.

"It's not like I can go to the dance now anyway, so you just wasted your money."

Beech picked up the ticket. I guess that's when she remembered he was sitting there.

Her bark softened. "Hey, kid." She ruffled his hair. Picked a piece of macaroni off his cape. "I have to go now, but I'll see you next time, okay?"

Beech nodded. "Net time."

She hiked her backpack up and stomped out the door.

I listened to her boots thunk down the steps.

What was *wrong* with her? Didn't she ever get tired of fighting with everybody?

And what was wrong with *me*? Why couldn't I have just kept my two extra quarters in my pocket?

Beech tried to smooth out the wrinkled ticket. He looked up at me, his face scrunched.

"I know. You think I scared her again." I shook my head. "Just eat your macaroni."

■ ■ ■

Later on, when I was leaning against the bathroom door, waiting for Beecher to get ready for bed, I spotted a spool of thread in the hallway. It had rolled into the corner, leaving a trail of pink thread behind it.

I followed the thread down the hall into my mom's room, across her rug, and under her desk, where the end of it was caught in the lid of the giant sewing box.

I lifted the lid to put it back. Inside was a mess. Who knew what Sam and Beech had been doing in there? Pink thread was mangled up everywhere. And bits of pink material.

And one more thing: My drawing of the sparkly superhero dress was gone.

twenty-three

I poked my fork at the edge of my chicken patty. Or, as Noah called it, my alleged chicken patty. We'd found very little evidence that the squishy gray slab was actual chicken.

I sneaked a quick glance across the lunchroom.

At Sam. Sitting under the EXIT sign. By herself. For the third day in a row.

Which was not my problem. Except, well, it kind of was.

I tore my mayonnaise packet open with my teeth, squirted it on the bun, and skooshed it around to coat the alleged patty.

Noah tapped his finger on my lunch tray. "You going to eat your fruit cup? You should. It's probably the only thing on your whole tray that contains a single nutrient. But if not . . . "

I pushed my tray toward him. "Go for it."

Noah scooped up the plastic cup of questionable fruit.

I shot another glance at Sam. Here was my problem: Her brother was suspended for stealing milk. Except he didn't steal it. And I was the only person who knew that.

So I should probably tell the truth. That's what H2O would do. Heck, that's what Beanboy would do (the real Beanboy, not me). He wouldn't even think about it. He'd go to the office, ask to see Mr. Petrucelli, and tell him exactly what happened on grilled cheese day in FACS.

It would be the right thing to do.

But I'd tried doing the right thing with the dance ticket. That hadn't worked out so hot for anybody.

Plus, if I told Mr. Petrucelli that Dillon *didn't* take the milk, I'm pretty sure I'd have to tell him who *did*. And even though I'm not a huge fan of Kaley C.—or either of the Kaleys—it would feel weird to be the person who got her kicked out of school instead of Dillon.

Especially if she found out who told on her.

Which she would.

And so would everyone else.

Including Emma.

And then the whole school would hate me.

First they'd find out I existed.

Then they'd hate me.

Including Emma.

Plus, if we're being honest, did anyone really want Dillon Zawicki tearing through the halls of Earhart Middle again any time soon?

Well, yeah. I could think of one person: his grandpa.

A picture flashed in my head of a really nice white-haired guy, crouched beside Beech, admiring his sorry pumpkin, giving him a rusty wagon to haul it around in. Sam said he already had enough to worry about. And he probably did, growing all those apples and beets and stuff.

Actually, I could think of two people: his grandpa and Sam. Eating with Dillon had to be better than eating by yourself.

If I thought about it hard enough (which I sincerely did *not* want to do but somehow couldn't stop myself), I could think of three, if you counted Beecher, because he didn't want Sam to be sad.

And I don't know what was wrong with me, but for some reason, I didn't, either.

So that made four.

twenty-four

Dear Mr. Petrucelli:

Being a principal must be hard work, having to make all the rules and then make everybody follow them and kick out all the people who don't, plus on top of that, figure out who's lying and who's telling the truth.

Luckily, I can help you with that. Because here's the truth: Dillon Zawicki didn't steal the milk from the FACS room. It was actually Kaley Crumm, but she didn't do it on purpose. It was an accident, mostly because Kaley Crumm is not very good at opening things.

See, she was trying to get the lid off her milk, but she dropped it in the sink, and you never want to use dishwater milk. Ms. Flanigan would subtract serious Ingredient Contamination points. So Kaley borrowed Dillon and Sam's milk, only she couldn't ask first because Ms. Flanigan was talking and I bet she didn't want to to interrupt a teacher. So she borrowed their milk and then I think it got stuck in her refrigerator by accident.

So it was all a big mistake. Kaley didn't mean to steal it, and Dillon didn't steal anything at all.

I hope this clears things up and makes your job easier.

Sincerely,
A Concerned Anonymous Citizen

I stopped by the office after computer lab and told Louise, our secretary, I had a sore throat. I tried to look sick and feverish. Also I coughed a couple times.

It must've worked because Louise clucked her tongue and said, "You really *don't* look good. No color in your face at all. Better go on back and see the nurse."

I felt bad, lying to Louise.

But not bad enough to keep from coughing and sniffling down the little hallway behind her desk, a clean, bright hallway that led to a whole nest of rooms in our school that hardly anybody ever saw: nurse's office, counselor's office, teachers' lounge, detention room.

And also Mr. Petrucelli's office.

I sidled up to his door and, after glancing around to make sure nobody was looking, slipped my letter underneath. Which was kind of hard because he had carpet on the other side, and I kind of had to wriggle and push it to get it through.

Then I slipped back down the little hallway and past Louise's desk.

"Thanks." I pushed through the door and out of the office.

twenty-five

Sam was sitting on our front steps when I got home from school.

I didn't see her at first. I was scooting along Polk Street, head down, watching my sneakers scuff across the pavement, the hood of my sweatshirt pulled up to ward off the cold and the world. Thinking about how it would be way easier to make Beanboy the greatest sidekick ever if I didn't keep running into Zawickis everywhere I went.

I stepped up onto our curb. Dropped my backpack. Leaned against the light pole to wait for Beecher's bus.

And there she was.

Sitting on the top step, hugging her knees to her chest, running her finger through the dirt on the sidewalk.

She must've heard my backpack thump. She looked up. She eyed me. I eyed her. Like a game of chicken.

I blinked first. "It's Friday," I said. "I don't have Art Club."

She rolled her eyes. "I'm not an idiot. I know how to read a calendar."

She rose to her feet. Heaved her backpack onto her shoulder.

"Dillon gets to come back to school Monday," she said.

I looked at her. "Really? That's good."

"Good?" She narrowed her eyes. "You think it's good?"

"Well . . . isn't it?"

"Yeah. But why do *you* think so? Nobody else does."

Man. What was *with* her? Couldn't she just babysit Beecher and leave me alone? She had to make a special trip over here on a day that wasn't even Art Club and yell at me about her brother, of all people?

She stood there, kind of hugging the strap of her backpack, staring at the sidewalk.

"I went to Mr. Petrucelli's office with my grandpa today," she said finally. "He showed us the note."

I froze.

Then remembered to say, "Note? What note?"

"Oh, for pete's sake, Beanboy." She rolled her eyes again. "Are you *always* this stupid? I'm sure Mr. Petrucelli's never going to figure it out, so you can relax, but I've seen enough of your dumb little stickies to know what your writing looks like."

"Oh." I swallowed. "*That* note."

"Yeah. *That* note."

"So." I cleared my throat. "You're not going to tell him? Mr. Petrucelli, I mean. You're not going to tell him who really wrote it?"

"No, I'm not going to tell him." She pierced me with a glare. "What kind of person do you think I am?"

Well, the kind of person who drowns comic books and rips down dance flyers and calls people Beanboy, for one thing.

And who also doesn't mind making happy faces on macaroni for my goober of a brother.

That kind of person.

"Anyway." She let out a breath, like she was letting air out of a balloon. "I guess Mr. Petrucelli talked to Kaley C., and she started crying—of course—and admitted the whole thing and said she was sorry, and now Mr. Petrucelli says she's honest and brave and he wished all his students could be as truthful as her, because he thinks she's the one who secretly wrote the note so that Dillon wouldn't get in trouble for something she did."

"You're kidding."

"I wish. So she gets to stay in school and not be suspended or even do detention or anything because Mr. Petrucelli says she's suffered enough. She's supposed to apologize to Dillon. I wouldn't put money on it. But at least he's not kicked out anymore."

I nodded.

She crossed her arms. Kicked her boot against our bottom step. "So now, what, you think you're some kind of superhero, the great Beanboy, saving the scrubby little farm family?"

"What? No. I'm not a . . . hero or whatever. I was just trying to help."

She kicked again. "Too bad you didn't help sooner, before we lost all that money."

What? I looked at her. "How was I supposed to help sooner? I didn't even know Dillon was in trouble till he got kicked out of school. It's not like you ever talk to me or anything."

"I didn't think you wanted me to talk to you."

"I didn't think you wanted *me* to talk to *you.*"

"I don't."

"Okay then."

She hiked up her backpack. Pulled her jacket around her like she was going to leave. But then she just kept standing there.

Which made *me* feel like leaving, which was just stupid because it was *my house.*

"So. Anyway," she said. "I just came by to tell you about Dillon, and also I wanted to say"—she kicked the step—"I just, I came by—" She closed her eyes. "I just wanted to say thank you. Okay?"

"Um. Sure." I nodded. "Okay."

"Good." She pushed past me. "Tell the kid I'll see him Monday."

She started off down the sidewalk. And then, I don't why, my mouth started saying stuff again.

"Um, Sam?" it said. "I bet you don't have to lose the money. Your grandpa had to pay for the milk, but now that Mr. Petrucelli knows Dillon didn't take it, he'll probably give it back."

She stopped, her back to me. "He already did." She didn't turn around. "But he can't give back the cauliflower. Or the turnips. Or the squash. That morning when Grandpa had to come down and get Dillon and it was storming and raining with the wind blowing like it could about take your head off? Well, it did. It took our heads off. While my grandpa was talking to stupid Mr. Petrucelli who wouldn't listen to anything Dillon said, the storm laid it flat, the corn, the beans, everything. And Mr. Petrucelli can't give that back."

She hiked up her backpack and scuffed off down Polk Street.

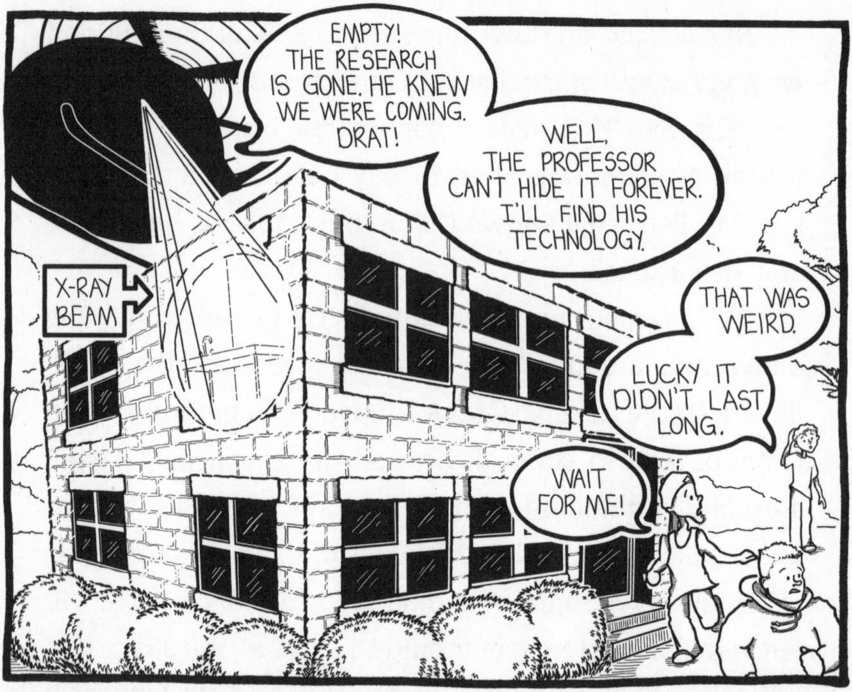
EMPTY! THE RESEARCH IS GONE. HE KNEW WE WERE COMING. DRAT!
WELL, THE PROFESSOR CAN'T HIDE IT FOREVER. I'LL FIND HIS TECHNOLOGY.
X-RAY BEAM
THAT WAS WEIRD.
LUCKY IT DIDN'T LAST LONG.
WAIT FOR ME!

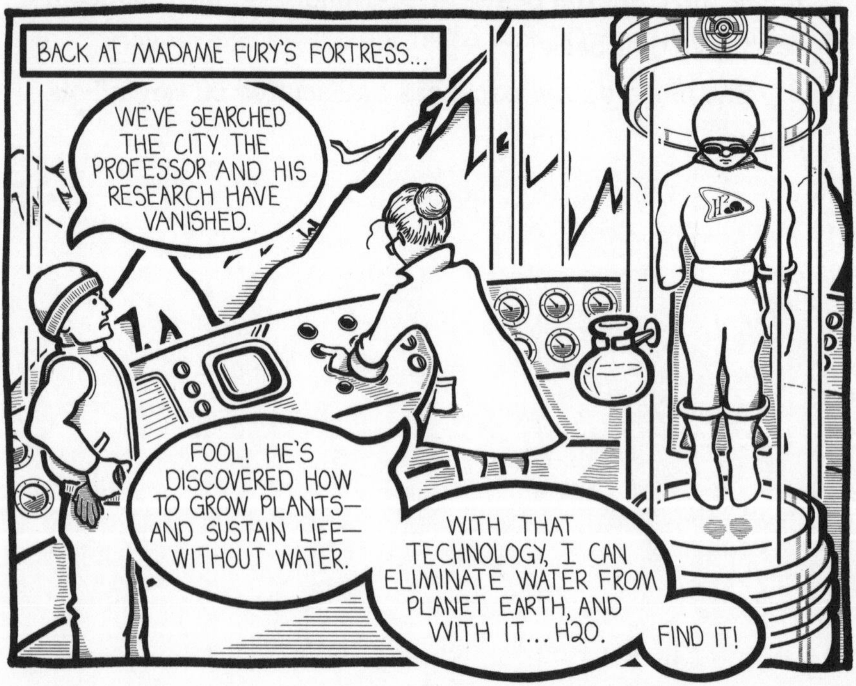
BACK AT MADAME FURY'S FORTRESS...
WE'VE SEARCHED THE CITY. THE PROFESSOR AND HIS RESEARCH HAVE VANISHED.
FOOL! HE'S DISCOVERED HOW TO GROW PLANTS— AND SUSTAIN LIFE— WITHOUT WATER.
WITH THAT TECHNOLOGY, I CAN ELIMINATE WATER FROM PLANET EARTH, AND WITH IT... H2O.
FIND IT!

twenty-six

Bing, bing. Bing, bing. Bing, bing.

I dragged myself from the Chasm of Sleep, fumbled for my alarm clock, and hit snooze. I collapsed back into my pillow.

Bing, bing. Bing, bing.

I groaned. The Batcave wasn't supposed to still be *bing*ing. I rubbed sleep crust from my eyes and realized the *bing* was coming from the other end of the house. I battled my bedspread to free my legs and stumbled down the dark hallway, feet slapping against the cold wood floor.

And found my mother sitting on the couch. Sort of. Mostly she was slumped against the arm of the couch, head buried in a clutter of papers, cheek pressed against the RETURN key of her laptop. Snoring like a freight train. I didn't even know she was home.

Carefully, so I wouldn't wake her, I peeled her face from the computer and slipped one of the couch pillows under her cheek, like a magician whipping a tablecloth from under a table full of china. The *binging* stopped. My mom mumbled and burrowed into the pillow.

I pushed aside a mountain of textbooks (A Comprehensive Analysis of Behavioral Statistics, 17th Edition—no wonder she was unconscious) and set her laptop on the coffee table. I was about to close the lid when I thought maybe I should save whatever she'd been working on. I didn't want to accidentally delete a term paper or something. My life wasn't perfect, but I wasn't ready for it to end.

I leaned down, finger hovering over the keyboard, all set to hit SAVE—

—and stopped.

Right there before my eyes, in giant glowing blue letters, were words I never thought I'd see on my mother's computer: "University Withdrawal."

That couldn't be right. My mother never quit anything. She still got newsletters from the Nancy Drew Fan Club she joined in fourth grade. If she wouldn't quit Nancy, she sure wouldn't quit school. Not after she'd been talking about going back to college for at least my whole life. Probably even before.

I shook my head. Her cheek must've clicked on the page by accident.

I crouched down for a closer look. It was instructions

for what to do if you decided to leave school. They even had an official list of Reasons for Withdrawal:

- Medical Issues
- Financial Hardship
- Personal Crisis
- Military Service
- Employment Conflict
- Family Burdens

Wow. That pretty much covered everything.

She had some other Web pages open, too. More stuff from the university. Some university foundation or something. I didn't look at them. I just closed her laptop. Made sure it was plugged in so she'd have plenty of battery.

I'd scattered some of her papers onto the floor when I whipped out the laptop. Now I gathered them up. I glanced through, trying to figure out what they were so I could maybe put them in the right order. They looked like class notes. And the beginning of a paper. Plus a note to herself, it looked like. A phone number and some scribbles:

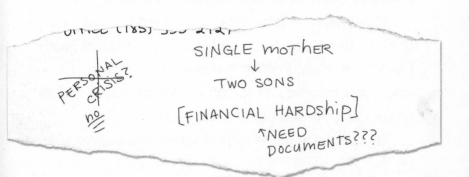

Which didn't make much sense. But then, two words that did:

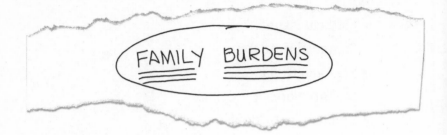

Family Burdens.
I sank back on my heels.
Family Burdens.

■ ■ ■

I crept back to my bedroom. Pulled out the sidekick contest entry form. Read through it. Made sure I'd spelled everything right, that my mom's name and address were neat and legible.

She'd brought home a package of big brown envelopes right after the day at the farmers' market. She'd used a couple, I think, but she still had a bunch left.

I liberated one from her desk, printed the contest address neatly on the front, and slid the entry form inside. I had to be ready. I couldn't waste time. As soon as I finished Beanboy, I would slip him in the envelope, seal the whole thing up, and put it in the mail.

He needed to get to the judges as soon as possible.

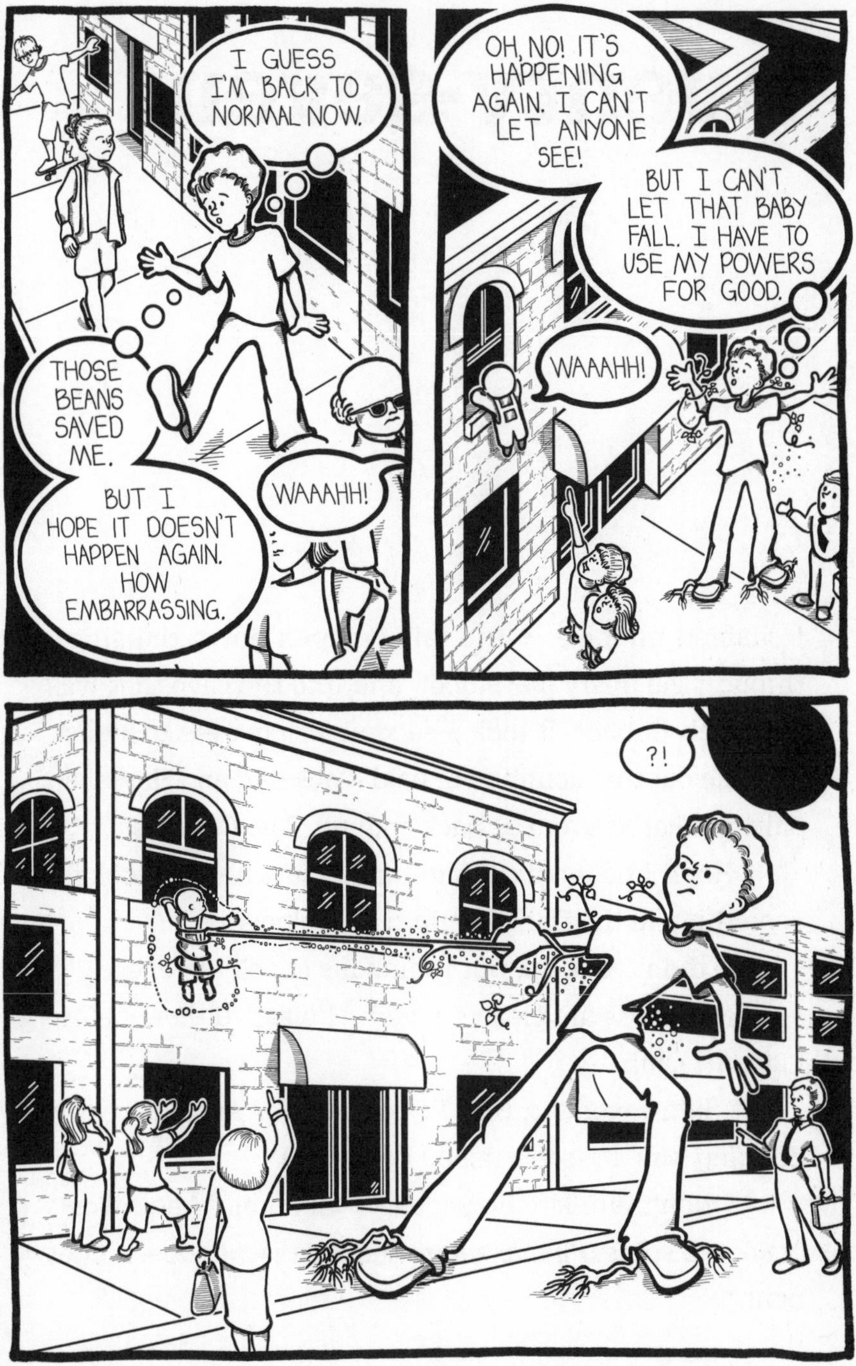
I GUESS I'M BACK TO NORMAL NOW.
THOSE BEANS SAVED ME.
BUT I HOPE IT DOESN'T HAPPEN AGAIN. HOW EMBARRASSING.
WAAAHH!
OH, NO! IT'S HAPPENING AGAIN. I CAN'T LET ANYONE SEE!
BUT I CAN'T LET THAT BABY FALL. I HAVE TO USE MY POWERS FOR GOOD.
WAAAHH!
?!

twenty-seven

I chained my bike to the rail. Scraped down the steps, through the dusty glass door, and into the cave that was Caveman Comics. It took a second for my eyes to adjust, to make out the mountain of wild black hair and Hawaiian shirt hunkered over the back counter. The Cavester.

"Hey," I hollered back to him. "I just need to look for something in the Dark Overlord encyclopedia."

He didn't look up. But I think his cheek twitched.

"My hands are clean," I said. "I washed them before I left Art Club."

(I didn't mention that I'd shot out of Art Club early, dodging Mrs. Frazee's raised eyebrow.)

"I won't wrinkle the pages," I told him. "And I won't crack the spine. I'll make sure the dust jacket doesn't get bent."

Caveman turned the page of his graphic novel. I took that as a yes.

I wove my way through the aisles to a tall, narrow shelf of books. Thumbtacked above was one of Caveman's dusty signs:

REFERENCE SECTION

I slid my finger over the thick spines. Past the Marvel encyclopedia. Past the DC encyclopedia. Past *Seventy Years of the World's Greatest Superheroes*.

My fingers stopped on a tall book at the end. I pulled it down. Ran my hand over the smooth cover. *The Dark Overlord Comics Encyclopedia: The Definitive Guide to the Characters of the Dark Overlord Universe.*

I balanced the weight of it in my hands. This was me. At least, it *could* be.

Or my mom could be, since officially, she was the one entering the contest.

Not just entering. Winning. Winning the contest.

She had to.

And I, her chief Family Burden, had to find Beanboy's

superhero heart so she wouldn't quit school. There had to be something here, in the *Overlord Encyclopedia*, that could help me. Something about H2O.

I settled on the floor, on Caveman's mismatched (and disturbingly crunchy) carpet, and opened the book in my lap. I leafed through the superheroes, sidekicks, and villains. Lumen-X. Lyonheart. The Mad Chatterer.

"Here." I found the entry and smoothed the page flat.

Case File: Madame Fury

Status: Supervillain

Base: Infuria, her laboratory fortress in the Himalayas

Superpower: Mad science

Superweapon: Stealth black helicopter, tricked out with laser beam, freeze beam, and other inventions that inflict pain and torture on anyone she believes has wronged her.

Real Name: Mary Ann Goodnight

Madame Fury was a major Overlord villain. They'd put in two whole pages about her. I started reading.

Mary Ann Goodnight was a clever, intelligent girl, even as a baby. Her parents, both brilliant scientists, were killed when their car skidded over an embankment during a storm. Three-year-old Mary Ann had been in the car, too. Hours later, rescuers found her, bruised and shaken, but otherwise unharmed.

Mary Ann was sent to live with her aunt, a kindly but poor woman who could not give young Mary Ann the education she needed. Mary Ann grew up wearing mended and well-worn hand-me-downs, teased and humiliated by classmates.

After working her way through college and finishing at the top of her class in science and mathematics, Mary Ann applied for a position at NAUTICA Enterprises, founded by renowned research scientist Marcus Poole. But Dr. Poole refused to hire her, saying her projects were too risky, that she hadn't gathered enough data on possible adverse effects. Mary Ann stormed out, taking her research plans with her and vowing to prove Dr. Poole—and anyone who had ever humiliated her—wrong. She built her own secret lab high in the Himalayas and took on a new identity: Madame Fury.

But when a tragic lab experiment at NAUTICA went horribly wrong, changing Marcus Poole's DNA structure forever, Madame Fury's quest to prove Dr. Poole wrong became that much more difficult. Wracked with guilt and grief over the accident, Marcus Poole became H_2O, vowing to use his powers to keep the planet safe.

Since that moment, Marcus Poole and Mary Ann Goodnight, alias H2O and Madame Fury, have been locked in a battle of good vs. evil, a battle that may well shape the future of Planet Earth.

I ran my finger down the entry. Most of it I already knew. I'd kind of forgotten about Madame Fury's whole childhood humiliation thing, so I scribbled it down in my notebook. It made sense. Explained how sweet Mary Ann Goodnight had snapped and turned into Madame Fury.

But I didn't see how it could help Beanboy.

I flipped to the middle of the encyclopedia. Found a tiny entry about Marcus Poole's assistant, Godfrey Mann:

**Case File:
Godfrey Mann**

Status: Faithful Assistant (not powerful enough to be considered a sidekick)

Base: NAUTICA Enterprises laboratory run by Dr. Marcus Poole

Superpower: none

Superweapon: none

Real Name: Godfrey Mann

Godfrey Mann appeared in the first H2O comic book, *Underwater Adventures,* long enough to die in the laboratory disaster that created H2O.

Godfrey, a man riddled with fears—of snakes, mud, germs, storms—became paralyzed by the violent thunderstorm unleashed by the disaster. Dr. Poole, trying to rescue his assistant, was struck by underwater electrical currents caused by the storm, which changed the structure of his DNA, turning him to water and giving him aqueous superpowers. Because Dr. Poole was unable to save Godfrey, he vowed to use his new powers to keep the planet safe, dedicating his quest to the memory of his faithful lab assistant.

I sighed again. I didn't see how any of this stuff about some lab assistant nobody even remembered was going to help. I scribbled it in my notebook anyway, then turned to the H2O entry. I'd read it before, all four pages, roughly a million times. I didn't find anything new.

I slid the Overlord encyclopedia back on the shelf (pages unwrinkled, spine uncracked, dust cover completely straight).

"Thanks," I hollered to Caveman.

Caveman, still buried in his graphic novel, grunted. I think.

I pushed out of the cave and up the steps, squinting

against the sudden bright light. I unlocked my bike and pedaled away. Past the flickering Caveman sign. Toward Weaver's. Toward the mannequins under their sign: FALL DANCE DRESSES!

I pedaled along, picking up speed, thinking maybe, if I could get Beech to watch cartoons, I could sneak into my room and work on Beanboy.

The late afternoon sun glinted off the Weaver's window, turning the dresses into a glimmering blur of color—blue, pink, lavender, orange.

And on the end, red.

With straps.

And sparkles.

I nearly rammed into a parking meter.

I wobbled to a stop. Climbed off my bike. Rolled it over to the Weaver's window.

I pressed my hands against the glass. Squinted. Squinted some more.

The more I squinted, the more I was sure. Sam's drawing, the not very excellent one with the eraser hole in the armpit? It was exactly the same as the red dress in the Weaver's window.

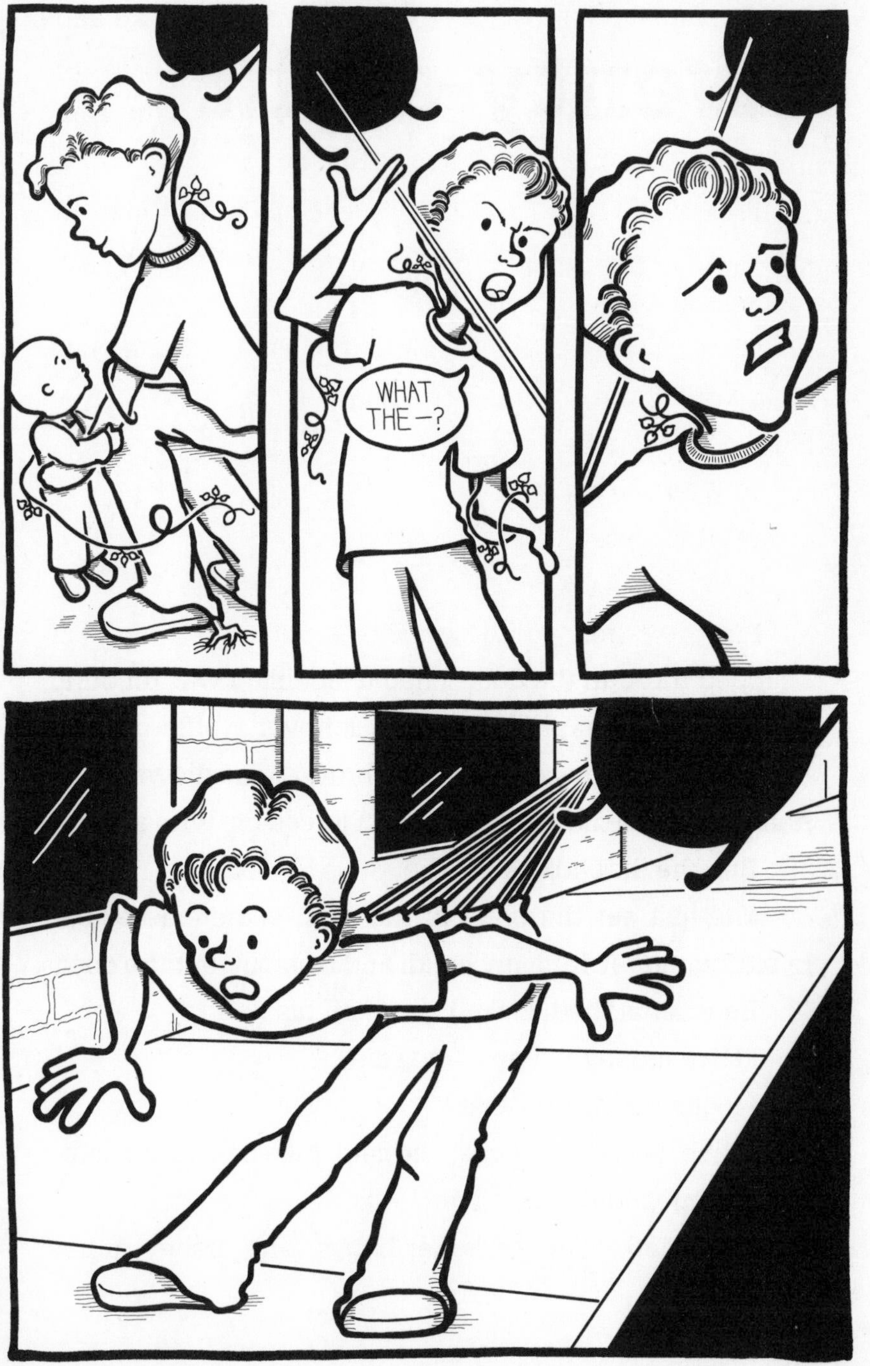
WHAT THE—?

twenty-eight

I slipped through the door. Tried to act like I was on time.

Sam was scraping Beecher's leftover waffle crumbs into the trash. She cocked an eyebrow at the glowing red numbers on the microwave: 5:03. Pierced me with a glare.

But she didn't bark.

She just set the plate in the sink, snatched her babysitting money from my hand, and tromped out the door.

Beecher sighed. Licked syrup off his hand.

"Give money to Papa," he said.

I looked at him. "What?"

"Give. Money. To *Papa*," he said. Like he was explaining to somebody slow.

I frowned. "She gives her babysitting money to her grandpa?"

"Has to." He held his hands out. "No beans. No tune-up."

I thought about that for a second. "You mean turnips? No turnips?"

He nodded again. "No beans. No tune-up. No dress." He let out a big breath. "Life suts."

Yeah. Sometimes it did.

I scrubbed the syrup off and set him in front of the cartoon channel.

And then what I should've done was, I should've marched into the Batcave and pulled out the Bristol board I'd brought home from Art Club. I should've started working on Beanboy before Beech came in to bug me.

So that's what I decided to do.

Except first I slipped into my mom's room. I tiptoed across the rug, knelt down to slide the sewing box out from under the desk—

—and noticed something pink stuffed into the waste-basket. Something fluffy and pink that filled the whole basket and spilled over the side. Something fluffy and pink and billowy that hadn't been there before.

I pulled it out. Kept pulling and pulling. Pulled till I had an entire pink armful of . . . dress. Except I was holding it upside down. I think. And partly inside out. I turned it over and gave it a shake. Held it up.

It was some kind of fancy dress. The kind you'd wear to a dance maybe. Not a dance *this* century, except maybe for Halloween.

And only if you were a zombie. Because somebody'd taken scissors to the whole top part of it. Chopped off the fluffy sleeves, which—I glanced into my mom's trash— were lying dead at the bottom of the wastebasket. Tried to sew on some straps. Which were kind of bunched up and bumpy and not exactly the same length and not quite in the right place.

And the thing was, I recognized that dress.

I'd seen it before. The exact same dress. Outside Caveman. When Sam was standing in front of the Weaver's window. When she drowned my comic book so I wouldn't notice her grandpa carrying it out of the thrift store in an old paper bag.

"We try. Just touldn't."

I turned. Beech was standing in the doorway.

"You and Sam?" I said. "This is what you've been up to?

He nodded. "Try to sew." He held up his hands, then dropped them to his sides. "No good."

That part sure was true. When it came to sewing, Beecher and Sam were pretty much no good.

Beech and I stood side by side, squinting at the chopped-up, cockeyed, old pink dress. Beech crawled under the desk and dug a wadded-up ball of paper out from under the dead pink sleeves in the trash can.

"Posed to be this." He unballed the paper. Smoothed it out along the edge of the desk and handed it to me.

It was my drawing. My drawing of the sparkly dress.

I held it up next to the pink dress. Looked at them side by side. Sam had been trying to turn an old dress from the thrift store into the sparkly dress from the Weaver's display window.

■ ■ ■

I put the dress back in the trash. I folded it first, carefully tucking in the bunched-up straps. Don't ask me why. I mean, it was just going to get set on the curb with the rest of the trash Monday morning, so it really didn't matter.

But it didn't seem right to just stuff something somebody'd been working that hard on into a trash can all wadded up. Especially not something somebody's grandpa had gotten for her in the first place.

Come to think of it, it didn't seem right to put it in the trash at all, even nicely folded.

I pulled it back out. Which didn't make any sense. Because clearly, Sam didn't want it anymore, and I sure didn't need a dusty old cut-up dress.

I got a plastic grocery sack from the kitchen, slid the dress inside, and tucked the whole thing behind my computer, under the poster, next to the pickle jar.

And then—finally—I did what I should've done in the first place and pulled out the Bristol board. Beanboy had to be in the mail and on his way to the contest judges by midnight Monday, which gave me less than four days to turn him into the greatest sidekick ever. All this Zawicki stuff had gotten me way off schedule.

I looked over my notes.

Mary Ann Goodnight.

Madame Fury.

Godfrey Mann.

H2O.

Beanboy's gassed-up superpowers.

There was something there. Some . . . clue. I could feel it.

I swiveled in my chair. Caught a glimpse of the pickle jar, which I'd barely thought about since I started drawing Beanboy. I dug it out from under the poster. Ran my thumb over the paper taped to the front. $61.24.

I looked at the sack of pink dress and slid open my drawer. Pulled out the wrinkled dance ticket I'd tried to give Sam. Smoothed it out on my desk.

Sam wanted a dress. Not an old pink out-of-style, do-it-yourself dress for zombies from the thrift shop. A new, sparkly red dress, with straps, from Weaver's Department Store, that she could wear to the Fall Fling and find out what it was like to wear the same kind of clothes as everybody else, even though she said she never wanted to.

Except that a gallon of milk and big gusting thunderstorm wiped her out and she ended up giving her money to her grandpa instead.

I shook my head. What was I doing? Beanboy had to be in the mail by Monday.

Monday.

Four and a half days from now.

I pushed the jar and the sack into the corner and pulled the poster down over them. I didn't have time for Sam Zawicki's dress problems. Even if I knew what to do about them.

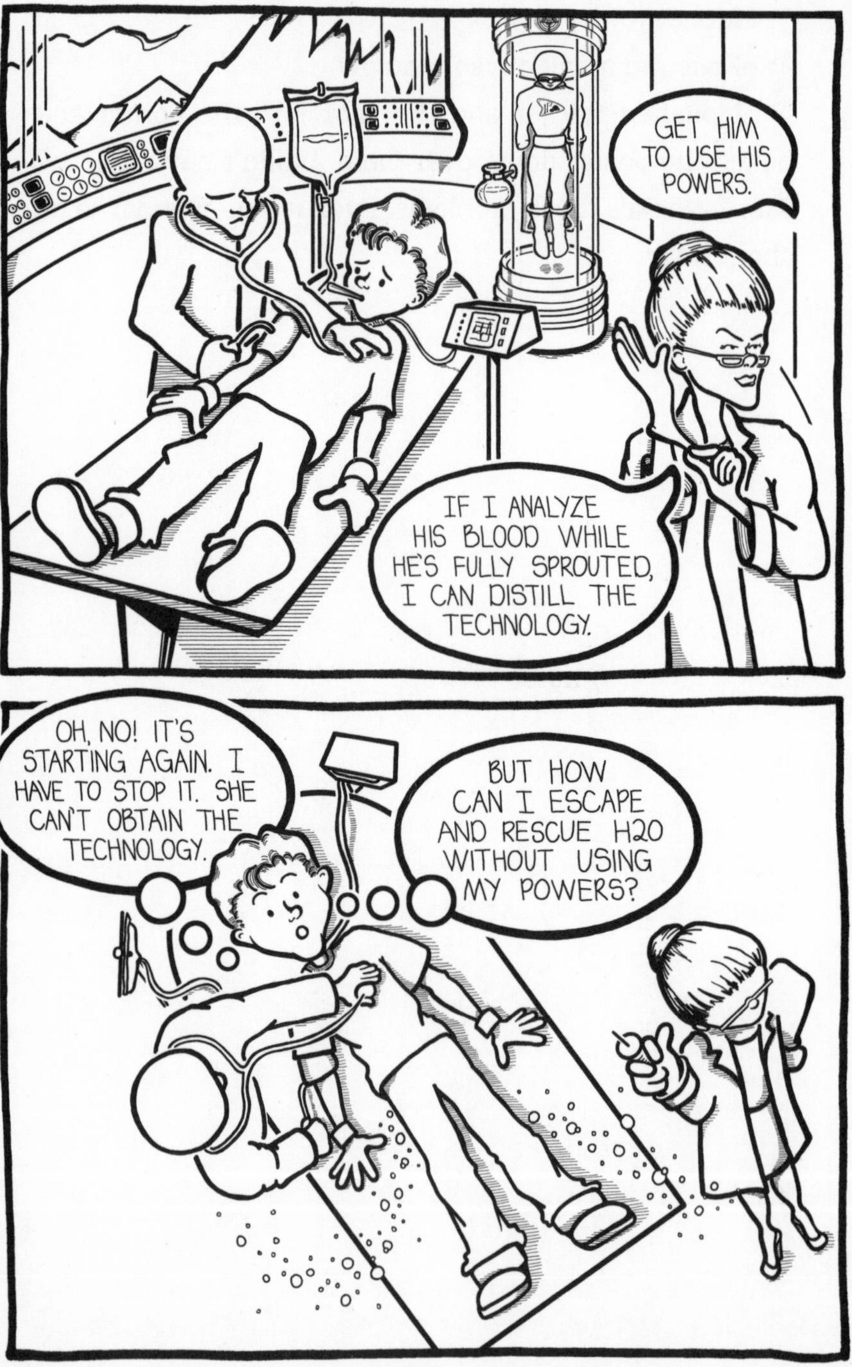
GET HIM TO USE HIS POWERS.
IF I ANALYZE HIS BLOOD WHILE HE'S FULLY SPROUTED, I CAN DISTILL THE TECHNOLOGY.
OH, NO! IT'S STARTING AGAIN. I HAVE TO STOP IT. SHE CAN'T OBTAIN THE TECHNOLOGY.
BUT HOW CAN I ESCAPE AND RESCUE H2O WITHOUT USING MY POWERS?

twenty-nine

I huddled at our lunch table, ignoring my lunch tray, sketching in my notebook.

Around me, Earhart Middle crackled with excitement. Tomorrow was the Fall Fling, and Emma and the Kaleys were spending their lunch period stringing up balloons and glittery stars to get the cafeteria ready. Emma unrolled a banner that said WELCOME TO THE FALL FLING! in tempera paint. The Kaleys twisted blue and silver crepe paper into long streamers and taped them along the wall over the trash cans.

And I'm sure they didn't notice, and probably wouldn't care if they did, but while they twisted and taped, Sam pierced them with a Zawicki Glare of Bad Luck and Ruination.

Now that Dillon wasn't kicked out anymore, he was

back to eating lunch at the Zawicki table under the EXIT sign. He chowed his sandwich, slugged down his milk, then ambled from the cafeteria, shooting a three-pointer at the trash can with his lunch sack on his way out. It bounced wide, but he didn't go in for the rebound. He left it lying on the floor and clanked out the door.

Sam crumpled her sack and got up to follow him.

And on her way to the trash can, she very calmly, very quietly, and with a lot more stealth than I ever knew she had, ran her finger along the wall of streamers, popping the Scotch tape loose from each one.

She was out the door and down the hall before the Kaleys started squealing.

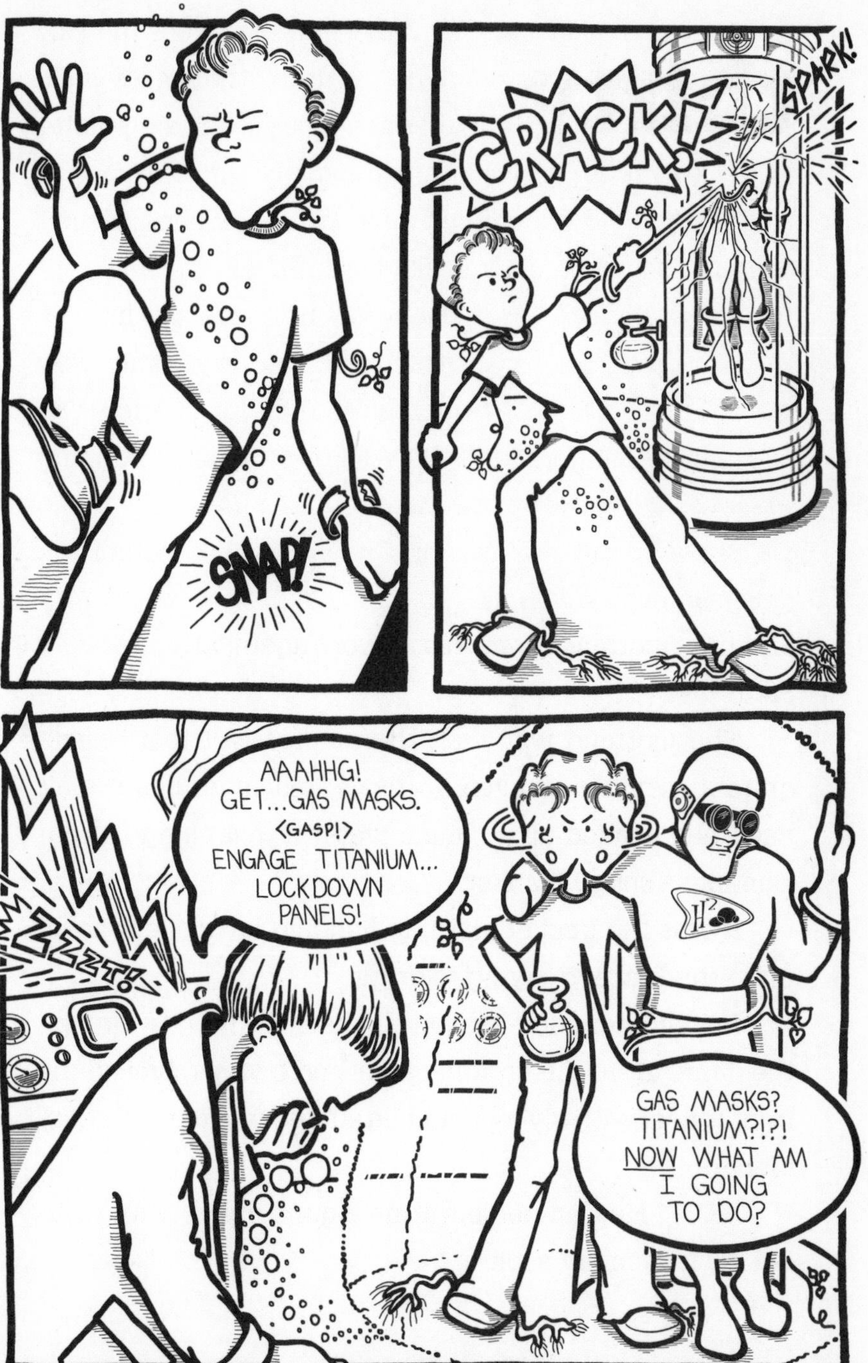
SNAP!
CRACK!
SPARK!
ZZZT!
AAAHHG! GET...GAS MASKS. <GASP!> ENGAGE TITANIUM... LOCKDOWN PANELS!
GAS MASKS? TITANIUM?!?! NOW WHAT AM I GOING TO DO?

thirty

Saturday morning Mom was at work again, just like every Saturday.

The morning was wet, the kind of wet that wasn't quite a sprinkle, or even a drizzle, but more like the air itself had soaked up so much water it just clung to your skin like a soggy blanket.

It was the kind of morning I should have spent holed up in the Batcave, trying to draw.

Instead, for some reason, I wheeled my bike through the damp air to the bottom of our porch steps, braced the front wheel with my foot, and lifted Beecher onto the handlebars.

"NO!" He clamped his arms around my neck and buried his face in my neck.

He didn't like riding on a bike any better than he liked going up and down stairs. And he wasn't any better at it, either.

"Beech," I rasped. My Adam's apple was pinned down by his elbow. "Let go."

He clenched tighter.

I wrangled his elbows around so I could at least swallow and pushed his head far enough to the side so that I could see, a little bit anyway. And that's how we rode to Weaver's Department Store: his butt perched on the handlebars, his arms clamped around my neck, his screechy little voice squealing, "No tip over! No tip over!" in my ear, his soggy pillowcase cape flapping in my face.

Halfway down Polk, I started seeing spots. I don't think I was getting enough oxygen.

All I can say is, it was probably a good thing Caveman shot down my big comic book delivery idea.

When I finally got us pedaled across town to Weaver's, I peeled Beecher off the handlebars. And off my neck. I locked my bike to a parking meter and dragged Beech inside.

You know how, when it's cold outside and you've been cleaning out the garage or raking leaves or something till you've worked up a sweat, so that you're this little island of hot in the middle of the cold, and the steam just rolls off you, right through your clothes, till you can feel the white fog rising off your head?

That was me and Beech as we stood in the middle of Weaver's first floor, trying to figure out how we were supposed to do this.

I'd thought about it all last night (the pink dress wouldn't let me think about much else) and this morning I rustled Beech out of bed early, shoveled oatmeal (with a raisin face) down his throat, and dug through the couch and all our chairs and in the pockets of the dirty clothes in our laundry hamper and in the junk drawer in the kitchen till I'd rounded up every last bit of money in the MacBean Family Apartment.

Then I strode into my room.

Where I should've kept working on Beanboy. Where I should've been getting him ready to mail to the contest judges. Where I *shouldn't* have reached under the poster behind my computer and pulled out the pickle jar.

Beech had followed me, his face scrunched in a suspicious frown.

"What doing?" he said.

I gripped the lid. "We need the money."

"NOOOOOOOO!" He launched himself at the jar. Wrapped his hands around it, his fingers suctioned to the glass like ten little tentacles.

"Beech. Listen." I tried to pull the jar away. "We've been saving our money for two months, and look." I tried to get him to see the paper taped to the front. "This is all we've got."

He clung to the jar. "Mom's money."

"But it's not enough. It's never going to be enough."

"No."

"Just listen—"

"No!"

"It's for Sam."

He loosened his grip. "Sam?"

I nodded.

He handed me the jar.

I emptied it out and stuffed the money in my pocket with the change from our couch.

And now here we stood, in Weaver's Department Store.

And I just about turned around, right then and there, and walked back out again.

But we'd been standing there long enough, steamy and wet in the middle of their clean, polished department store aisle, that I guess the Weaver's people started to get nervous, because suddenly a lady in a crisp blue suit, wearing her name—Suzanne—on a shiny gold nametag, hovered over us.

"May I help you?" she said, in a voice that sounded like we probably needed more help than she could provide, but she'd give it a shot.

"Yes." My voice kind of screeked out. I cleared my throat. Lowered my voice till I sounded like my dad. With a cold. And allergies. And maybe some bubonic plague. "Yes," I said. "We need this dress, in this size."

I'd checked the label inside the old pink thrift store

dress and written the size on my crumpled drawing of the sparkly dress. Now I showed both of them to Suzanne.

"It's the red one. In the window," I said. "It's for—for our—for—"

"Sam," Beech said, helpfully.

"We have money," I added, just in case Suzanne was worried.

She looked at me, then at the drawing, then at me again. Then she smiled, gave a sharp nod, and herded us through racks and shelves to a display of glittery dance dresses along the wall. She flipped through the display, peered down at the size scribbled on the drawing again, and pulled one out.

She held the hanger in one hand and draped the dress over her arm. The red sparkles flickered under the bright store lights.

I narrowed my eyes. Held my hands up to sort of measure it in my head, to make sure it would fit somebody who usually lumbered around in a big flapping army jacket and boots.

Finally I nodded. "That's the one."

And then I remembered.

A little white tag dangled from the dress. I took a breath, picked it up, and twisted it around so I could see the price.

"Oh," I said.

Dance dresses turned out to be way more expensive than I ever thought. Beech and I could scrape through all the change returns in all the Laundromats in all of Wheaton and still not have enough.

"Sam dress?" said Beech.

I shook my head.

Suzanne looked down at me, a smile on her face. "You didn't see the sale, did you?" She tipped her head toward a red and white sign above the dress display:

Fall Dance Dresses
50% off!

I stared at the sign. My mouth fell open. I'm sure I looked like a guppy.

"We need to get rid of the fall dresses," she said. "To make room for winter coats."

Beech squinched up at me. "Sam dress?"

I nodded. "Sam dress."

thirty-one

I didn't know very many dress salespeople. Actually, counting Suzanne, I knew one. But of all the dress salespeople in all the world, she was my favorite.

She rang us up, slid the dress into a giant white plastic bag, and tied it at the bottom so it wouldn't get splashed. The hanger poked out the top, and Suzanne showed me how to hold it so the dress wouldn't fall off.

Luckily, I didn't have to carry it far. The farmers' market was on the street behind Quincy, two blocks down. We walked my bike through the blanket-damp morning, me holding the dress bag up so it wouldn't drag the ground, and wheeled into the farmer's market parking lot.

And that's when the total stupidity of this plan hauled off and slapped me in the face.

Most people would probably think that, for a thirteen-year-old kid, buying a girl's dress would be the hard part. Because that's what I would've thought.

And lots of people would think riding Beecher all the way from our house on my bike, through the damp and the cold and the puddles and the flapping cape, with hardly any eardrums left after all the screaming, would be another hard part. And I would've thought that, too.

But that stuff was easy compared to what I had to do next: walk up to Sam Zawicki, the girl who about snapped my head off when I tried to give her a measly dance ticket, and hand her a whole, entire dress.

Clearly, I had not thought this through.

"Well. We're here now." I took a breath. "Let's get this over with."

Beech nodded. "Over with."

We wove our way through the aisles and stalls of the farmer's market, me and Beech and the bike and the dress, my arm about to fall off from holding it up. We reached the rickety pickup truck. Sam's grandpa stood out front, smiling and friendly, just like before.

But his forehead was wrinkled into a tough little knot, and you didn't have to be a genius to see why. The duct-taped boxes, piled high with vegetables a few weeks ago, now wilted in the morning dew, barely half full. Some potatoes. A few apples. A couple lonely eggplants. That was about it.

He spotted us standing there.

"Hey there, fella." He crouched down beside Beech. "How's that fine-looking pumpkin of yours?"

Beech about smiled himself in half. "Good," he said. "Sam help me."

"Yep." Sam's grandpa nodded. "That's what she said. She said the two of you are going to carve that pumpkin into a jack-o'-lantern once Halloween gets closer. A scary one, I hear."

Wow. That was news to me.

Beech scrunched his face. "Not real tary. Little bit tary."

"A little bit scary. Yep. Those are the best kind."

While they discussed the pumpkin, I formulated a second, better plan.

Because I knew what Sam would do. Even though she wanted that dress, so much she was willing to come to my house and babysit Beecher to earn money for it, no way she'd take it. She'd throw it back in my face, just like she threw the dance ticket. She'd rather give back something she really wanted than have to say thank you for it.

But she wasn't here right now. So maybe I could be nice before she found out.

Her grandpa stood up, his knees popping from being crouched down so long.

I held out the dress bag.

He cocked an eyebrow. "What's this?"

"For Sam," said Beech.

"Samantha?" Her grandpa poked a work-gnarled finger into the hole at the top and peeked inside. He gave a whistle. "That sure is one heap of sparkles." He looked up. Pushed the bag toward me. "Must've cost a heap, too. It's too much."

"No. Take it." I backed away from him. "Please. It's the one she wanted, plus you have no idea what I had to go through to get it."

He gave the dress another look. "She'd sure look pretty in a dress like that." He ran a hand over his mouth, like he was trying to make a hard decision.

I didn't give him a chance to make it. I reached into my shoe, pulled out the crinkled dance ticket, and stuck it in his hand.

Then I latched on to Beecher's elbow, turned my bike around, and wheeled out of the farmer's market.

Amelia M. Earhart Middle School

Fall Fling

$1.50

October 13
Admit One

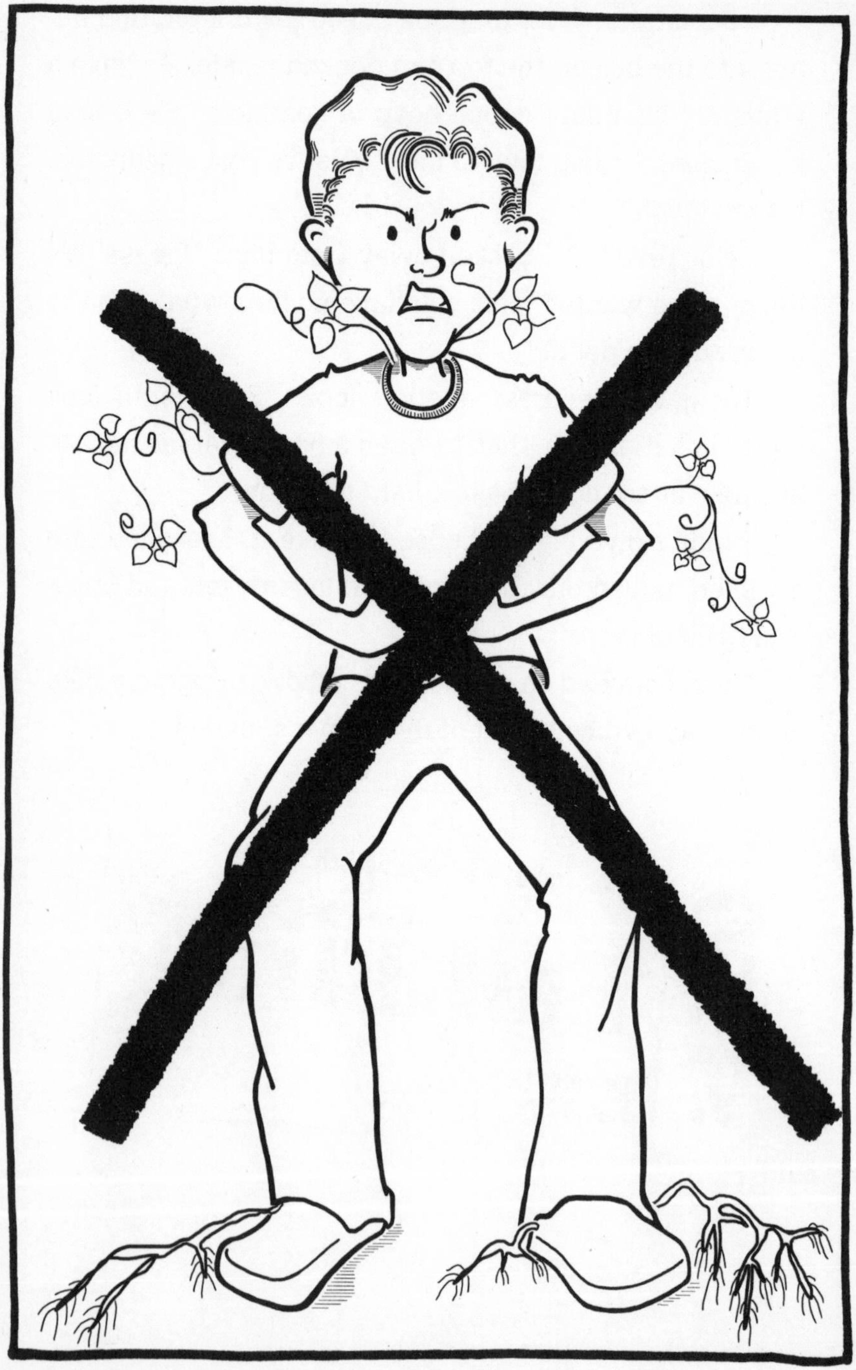

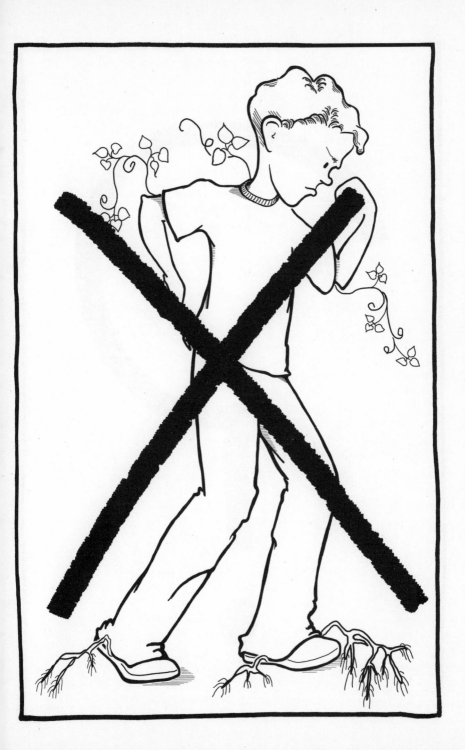

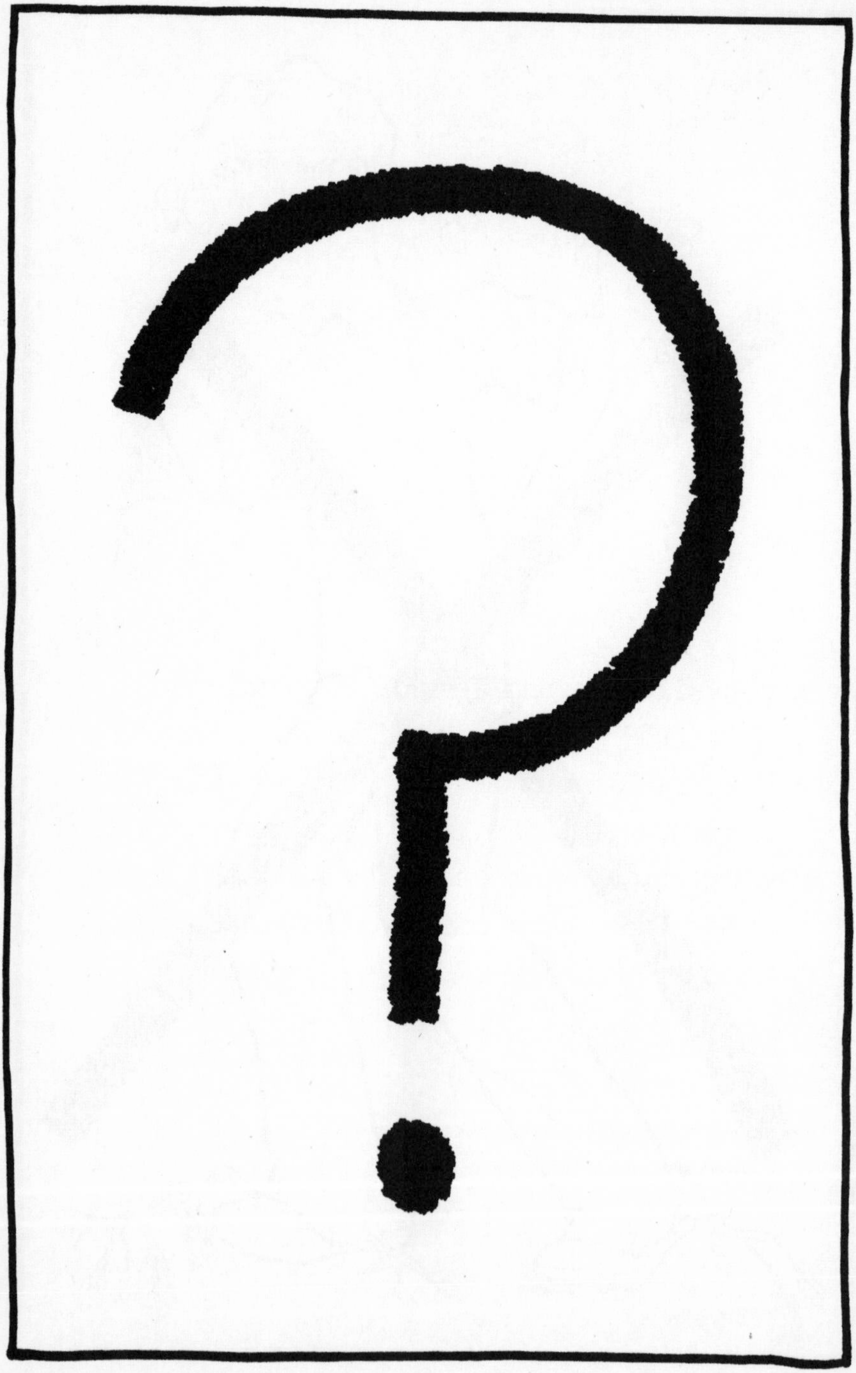

thirty-two

I crumpled the drawing. Tossed it at my trash can.

It bounced wide. I didn't go in for the rebound.

I slumped in my chair.

I had two days. One, really, since Monday I'd be in school all day, where my teachers would probably think I should do, I don't know, schoolwork or something.

I ran my finger over the contest instructions.

H2O's sidekick must possess the true heart of a hero. Reach deep within yourself, find that heroic heart, and create a sidekick who can rank among the greatest sidekicks in comic book history.

One day.

One day to find a superhero heart.

thirty-three

We stood under the blue and silver WELCOME TO THE FALL FLING! banner, me and Noah, behind the snack table, within easy reach of the popcorn and fruit punch.

The lights were turned down low. A twirly ball hung from the ceiling, sending flicks of light shooting across the lunchroom. Music pumped from the stereo system Coach Wilder had rolled in from the gym. The faint aroma of bleach water and old chicken nuggets drifted about the edges of the room.

We munched our popcorn. Noah tapped his foot to the music. I gave my armpit a covert sniff, just to make sure my sport-scent deodorant was working. So far it was.

I wasn't in much of a dancing mood, to tell you the truth. If I hadn't already promised Noah, I probably wouldn't have even come. I probably would've stayed home with my Bristol board and marker, filling my trash can with more useless drawings.

Emma skittered up, her shiny dress and shiny personality and shiny gold glitter hairspray nearly blinding us. I barely even noticed the Kaleys, following along in her wake.

"This is a disaster," she whispered. Even in a whisper, her mind-jamming superpowers beamed down on us like a force field.

"Oh, I don't think so." Noah glanced around. "You did a good job with the decorations. The flickery light's a sweet touch. And the popcorn's crunchy."

"But this is a *dance*," said Emma. "And nobody's dancing."

We nodded. All the girls, in their new dance dresses, huddled in clumps on one side of the cafeteria. All the guys, hands stuffed in their pockets, trying to look too cool to be here, huddled in clumps on the other side. The clumps eyed each other. But nobody had worked up the gumption to cross the wide stretch of lunchroom linoleum and actually dance.

Noah shrugged. "Nobody's dancing yet," he said. "But they will."

Emma sighed. "I hope you're right."

She'd been shooting frantic glances at the clumps of nondancing people. Now she stopped, a really surprised look on her face. She stared at the door.

"Wow," she said. And not in a mean way.

I turned.

Standing inside the door was a girl.

A girl who normally didn't walk like a girl or talk like a girl or punch people like a girl.

A girl who normally wore an army surplus jacket flapping around her about five sizes too big.

A girl who actually . . . looked like a girl.

In a sparkly dance dress.

With her hair, well, *fixed*. In some kind of braid or something. Not flying around like it was on fire.

Wearing combat boots.

She must've polished them, because they gleamed black in the flickery lunchroom light. And I'm no fashion designer, but with the red sparkles and everything, those boots looked . . . perfect.

She stood right inside the door, arms crossed, glaring at pretty much everybody, glaring at the balloons and paper streamers, and especially glaring at the twirly glitter ball, like she was just waiting for it to start something. For a second I was afraid she was going to turn around and stomp back out. Then she shook her braided head, lifted her chin, and strode across the cafeteria to the snack table.

She saw me and pierced me with a Zawicki Glare of Don't-Look-at-Me-Don't-Talk-to-Me-Don't-Come-Within-a-Mile-of-Me-Beanboy-I'm-Not-Kidding-I-Will-Kill-You.

So I pierced her back with a Tucker MacBean Glare of Fine-Because-That-Was-My-Plan-Too. Only she missed it because she wasn't looking at me anymore.

Noah, being Noah, hadn't even noticed Sam walk in. He was still focused on Emma and the dance problem.

"Everybody just needs time to get warmed up," he was saying. "Nobody goes out to dance right away. Nobody wants to be first."

Emma shook her head. "We don't have time to wait for people to warm up. The dance is over at nine. And you know Ms. Flanigan." She shot a glance at our FACS teacher, who was circling the cafeteria, clipboard and pencil at the ready. "If we don't get somebody dancing soon, she'll never let another seventh-grader within a mile of the planning committee." She shook her head. "I'm letting the whole seventh grade down."

"No, you're not," said Noah. "That's crazy. You just need to give this thing a jump-start. Get somebody to dance with you." He motioned his head toward me. "Once people see you out there"—he motioned again—"they'll go out, too, and pretty soon everybody'll be dancing."

Noah tipped his head again, and Emma could take a hint, I guess, because her eyes got big and she latched onto my arm.

"Yes!" she said, her hand sizzling a warm, toasty spot into my skin. "You guys are the best. I knew you'd know what to do. Come on, Tuck." She tugged my arm. "Let's give this thing a jump-start."

"Ah—urr—guk," I said.

Noah stuck a finger into the middle of my back. Pushed me forward. "Go. Emma needs you." He lowered his voice. "And for pete's sake, say something besides 'guk.'"

I nodded, pushed my popcorn bag at him, and—while the Kaleys watched with their mouths hanging open—followed Emma across the cafeteria. I really couldn't help it. She still had a hold of my arm, and Emma's a lot stronger than she looks.

And I hate to admit this out loud, but even though it's hard to be invisible when you're standing under a twirly glitter ball, and even though I am hardly an excellent dancer, and even though my heart was thumping so loud in my ears I couldn't hear what song was playing, at that very minute, following Emma across the cafeteria was the exact one thing I wanted to do in the universe. Even if she hadn't been dragging me.

We got to the middle of the floor, and Emma turned and gave me her half-dimple smile. Her gold glitter hairspray glittered. Her eyes twinkled under the twinkly ball.

For that one small second, I'm pretty sure I passed out, right there in the middle of the Amelia M. Earhart Middle School cafeteria.

We started to dance. I think it was a fast song. I'm pretty sure I was actually dancing. Moving my arms and stuff, maybe even my legs. Not completely standing there like a stump.

And as I drifted back to consciousness, I found that Noah's brilliant plan was working. While I'd been passed out, other people had trickled over, till now the whole dance area was pretty crowded. Ms. Flanigan had tucked her clipboard under her arm, slid her pencil into her hair, and was drinking a cup of fruit punch.

It was easier to be invisible now that we weren't the only ones under the twirly glitter ball. Emma leaned in to say something to me, and I actually said something back. You know, formed words and everything.

Here's what she said. She said: "Oh, my gosh, I'm so relieved. I think the dance is going to turn out okay after all."

And I said: "Yeah."

The song changed, and I figured we were finished dancing, now that we'd saved the Fall Fling and everything. But Emma just changed beat with the music and kept dancing.

And remember that stuff about the zone? Suddenly there I was again. Smack in the middle of the zone. Dancing with the shiniest girl in all of Wheaton. For two whole songs in a row. Having a conversation. Kind of. Sport-scent deodorant locked and loaded.

I could hear the music now, and I danced along to the beat. Moved my legs. Bobbed my head. Snapped my fingers once. Then I got really crazy and did a little twirl.

And that's when I saw her.

Sam. She was still by the snack table. Only now she was surrounded by Kaleys.

And she was backing away from them, which was just . . . weird. Sam Zawicki never backed away from anything.

"Tuck?" Emma leaned in to shout in my ear, because the music was pretty loud. "Don't you like this song? You want to stop?"

I shook my head. I think maybe I said, "Guk." And started moving my legs again.

I shot a quick glance at the snack table.

And saw *why* Sam was backing away.

Kaley C. had stuck her fingertips in her cup of fruit punch, and she was flicking punch in Sam's direction. And with each flick, Sam took a step backward, her hands held up in front of her to shield the red sparkles.

I blinked. She wasn't backing away to save herself. She was backing away to save the dress.

And people were starting to watch.

I tried to start dancing again. But I kept glancing back at the snack table.

Emma touched my arm. "Are you okay?"

I looked at her. At all that shiny hair and shiny personality. At her hand, warm and toasty on my arm.

And my zone? At that very moment, it skidded into a pole.

"I—I just—I have to—" I flung an arm toward the snack table. "I'm sorry."

And I really was. I was probably the sorriest person I'd ever known.

Because when I turned and left the dance floor, I knew I was leaving it for good. After what I was about to do, Emma would never dance with me again.

Nobody would.

The whole school would hate me.

Including Emma.

I doubted even Noah would talk to me.

Nobody would. Probably not even the teachers.

I'd have to be homeschooled. Except since I'd be the only one home, I'd have to homeschool myself.

I walked across the cafeteria, under the flickering lights and the floaty balloons, one step after another, toward the snack table.

Toward my doom.

I seriously have no idea what is wrong with me.

As I got closer, I could hear Kaley C. A small crowd had gathered behind her.

"I know you're the one who told Mr. Petrucelli." Kaley C. flicked punch. "I know you're the one who got me in trouble."

"What? Are you kidding me?" Sam wiped specks of punch off her arm. "You didn't get in trouble. Mr. Petrucelli's probably going to give you an award."

"But you didn't know that." Flick. "You told him because you were trying to get me in trouble."

The crowd murmured in agreement.

Sam took a step back. "You got my brother in trouble for something he didn't do."

"What difference does it make?" Flick. Flick. "He's always in trouble for something. You'd think he'd be happy to stay home for a week. We were sure happy he was gone."

The crowd nodded and whispered.

I pushed my way through.

"You know what would make us really happy? If the Zawickis stayed home for good. We're tired of you causing trouble for everyone else. We're tired of—"

"It wasn't Sam."

A voice rang out, a voice that sounded disturbingly like . . . mine.

I swallowed. Stepped forward.

"Tucker?" Noah cut me a look. "What are you doing?"

Ending my life as I knew it.

I took a breath. "It was me," I told Kaley C. "I wrote the note to Mr. Petrucelli."

Kaley C., actually both of the Kaleys, actually the whole crowd, turned on me.

"You?" Kaley C. shook her head. "No way."

"Yes," I said. "Way."

"It couldn't be." She gave me a disgusted look, the kind of look you give a bug you just crushed under your shoe. "You never do anything."

"Yes, I do." I swallowed. "I did this. Because I saw what happened. In FACS."

"So *you* tried to get me in trouble?"

I could feel the crowd watching. Could feel them stabbing me with their pitchfork glares. Stabbing the traitor who ratted out Kaley C.

I could see Noah, still standing beside the snack table, mouth open, a really confused look on his face.

"No," I said. "I didn't try to get *anybody* in trouble."

Kaley C. narrowed her eyes. "Then why couldn't you just leave it alone?"

I could see the crowd narrowing its eyes, too. Nodding. Wondering why dweeby Tucker MacBean couldn't just stick to his own pathetic life and leave Kaley C. alone.

"It wasn't fair."

This was a new voice. A voice that sounded suspiciously like . . . Emma's?

I turned, and there she was. I steeled myself. Waited for her to stab me with her own pitchfork glare.

But she didn't.

She crossed her arms and leveled a look at Kaley C. "Maybe *you* think it's okay to stand by and watch somebody get in trouble for something he didn't do, but Tucker's not that kind of person."

She was standing there side by side with Sam, both of them standing by . . . me.

Yeah. Me, Sam, Emma. Like the Justice League from a twisted alternative universe.

Noah had a weird look on his face. Still, even though

he didn't have a clue what was going on, he moved over and stood beside us.

That was my friend, Noah Spooner. Confused, but completely loyal.

Emma was still looking at Kaley C. "This is a dance," she said, "and we worked really hard to put it together. So why don't we all go dance."

The crowd nodded and murmured and sort of drifted away. The Kaleys stared at Emma for just a second longer, then they turned and stalked away, too.

Emma grabbed Noah's arm. "Come on," she said. "Ms. Flanigan's looking. We better get out there."

And then all that was left was me and Sam. Standing by the snack table.

She folded her arms over her red sparkly dress. "Don't think I'm going to dance with you," she said. "'Cause I'm not."

"No problem," I said.

"Good."

"Good."

So we just stood there.

"Kind of weird," Sam said finally. She poked at a floor tile with her boot. "The Kaleys didn't even know who I was at first." She looked up. "Not very bright, huh? I mean, change the clothes, braid the hair, and suddenly nobody knows who I am?"

I nodded. "The Clark Kent syndrome."

She gave me a weird look.

I shrugged. "Like Clark Kent and the glasses. Take them off, he's Superman. Put them back on, nobody recognizes him."

"Yeah." She nodded. "When the Kaleys thought I was just some random girl, they treated me pretty much normal. Kaley C. even said, 'Oh, sorry,' when she bumped me with her elbow. She said it kind of snotty, but she said it. Then they figured out who I was, and suddenly they're looking at me like they always do, like—what did you call it? The loser dweeb look?" She toed the floor tile. "And I hadn't changed at all. I was still the very same person."

I nodded again. Inside, the same person. Outside, arch nemesis of the world.

I stopped.

Blinked.

Looked at her.

"That's it," I said. "That's the secret of Beanboy."

thirty-four

I raced from the cafeteria. Through the bowels of Amelia M. Earhart Middle School, my footsteps echoing down the dark, empty halls. I clanked out the front door into the crisp autumn night.

And I probably would've felt bad about leaving Noah there all by himself. Sam, too. Except here's the really weird thing: When I left, they were dancing. Together. Moving their arms and everything. Well, Noah was moving his arms. Sam was swaying. A little. Sort of. But she was out there. Under the twirly glitter ball.

I know. I was shocked, too.

I unlocked my bike, leaped onboard, and pedaled like a crazy person, a crazy blur under the streetlights of Wheaton. I skidded to a stop at our porch, lugged my bike into the entry hall, and thumped up the steps to the MacBean Family Apartment.

I burst into the kitchen.

Beech was perched on his chair, wearing the pillow-case. Mom was pulling corn dogs from the oven.

She looked up. "Tucker? Is the dance over already?" She glanced at the clock on the microwave. "I didn't expect you for another hour. Are you okay?"

"Fine." I leaned over, hands on my knees, breathing hard. "Great actually."

"Hey!" Beech bounced on the edge of his chair. "You home! We watch TV? We read eight-two-oh?

"Beech. Listen." I straightened up. "You want to see how Beanboy ends?"

He nodded.

"Okay. Then here's the deal. I'm going to my room, and I'm shutting the door, and I'm finishing the comic book. And you're staying out here. Okay? You can't come in. You can't bang on the door. You can't sit in the hallway and sing the Batman song till I can't stand it anymore and let you in. You can't bug me in any way till I'm finished. Got it?"

"Got it." He swiped his hands like an umpire calling a runner safe. "No. Bug. Anybody."

I looked at him.

"Don't worry, Tuck. He won't have time to bug anybody." Mom slid a corn dog onto a plate, drew a face on it with ketchup, and handed it to him. "The Beech-man and I have some cartoons to watch, don't we, Beech?"

Beech gazed up at Mom like she was a superhero.

And then her purse started to ring.

Dun. Dun. Dun. Dun duh-dun, duh-dun, duh-dun.

I froze. Beech froze. Mom froze.

We stared at her purse, hanging by the door.

Beech slumped back in his chair. "No bad news. No big bad news."

Mom groaned and reached for her phone.

"Don't answer it," I said.

She looked at me. "I have to."

"No, you don't. I'm serious. Say you didn't hear it. Say your phone was off. Say anything. Just don't answer."

"Tuck. You know I can't do that." She rummaged in her purse. "What if it's important?"

"It's always important. No matter what happens down at that bank, they always think it's important. Why do they always think they're more important than anything else?"

"Tucker." She closed her eyes. "They need me."

"I know," I said. "But we need you more."

Mom looked at me. She looked at Beech. She looked at the cell phone, quivering in her hand.

And she held the button down to shut it off.

"You're right." She tossed the phone back in her purse. "And you know what? I need you guys, too."

■ ■ ■

I left Mom and Beech and their happy-face corn dogs, while I holed up in the Batcave.

I fired up my computer.

My fingers started typing before I could talk them out of it.

To: BigBeanInBoston
From: SuperTuck
Re: Birthday Money—Really

Dad,

I like the four baseball bats I already have, and I appreciate everything you did to get them for me, but I don't need another one. For my birthday this year, I wasn't kidding. I really do want money. *I* do. Not Mom. Me. And if I end up giving my money to Mom for some reason, it's not because she asked me to. It's because I want to. Because the MacBeans are a family, and that's what families do. They stick together.

I hope that doesn't make you mad.

Love,
Tucker

I hit SEND.

Then I squared a clean crisp sheet of Bristol board on my desk and started to draw.

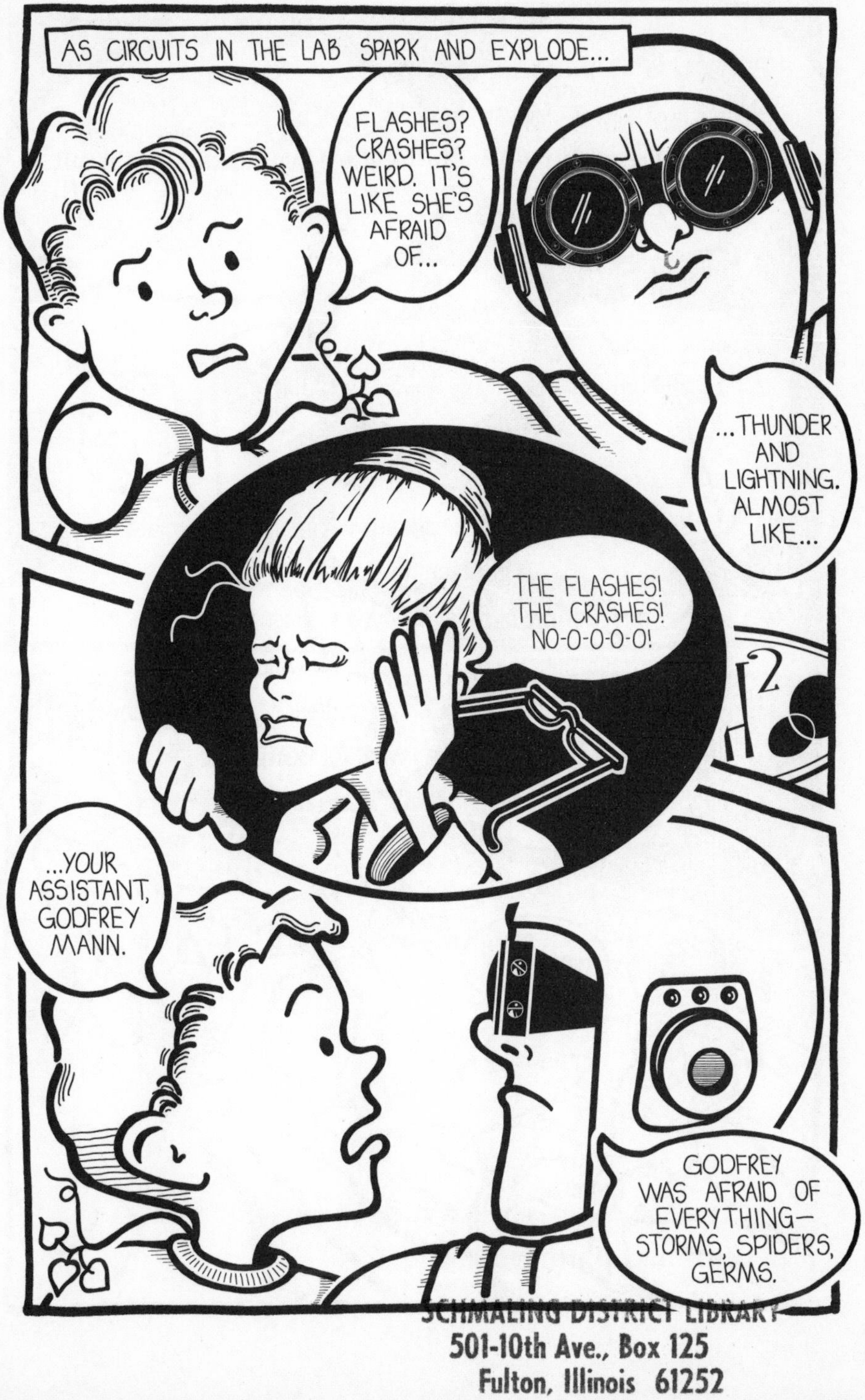
AS CIRCUITS IN THE LAB SPARK AND EXPLODE...
FLASHES? CRASHES? WEIRD. IT'S LIKE SHE'S AFRAID OF...
...THUNDER AND LIGHTNING. ALMOST LIKE...
THE FLASHES! THE CRASHES! NO-O-O-O-O!
...YOUR ASSISTANT, GODFREY MANN.
GODFREY WAS AFRAID OF EVERYTHING—STORMS, SPIDERS, GERMS.

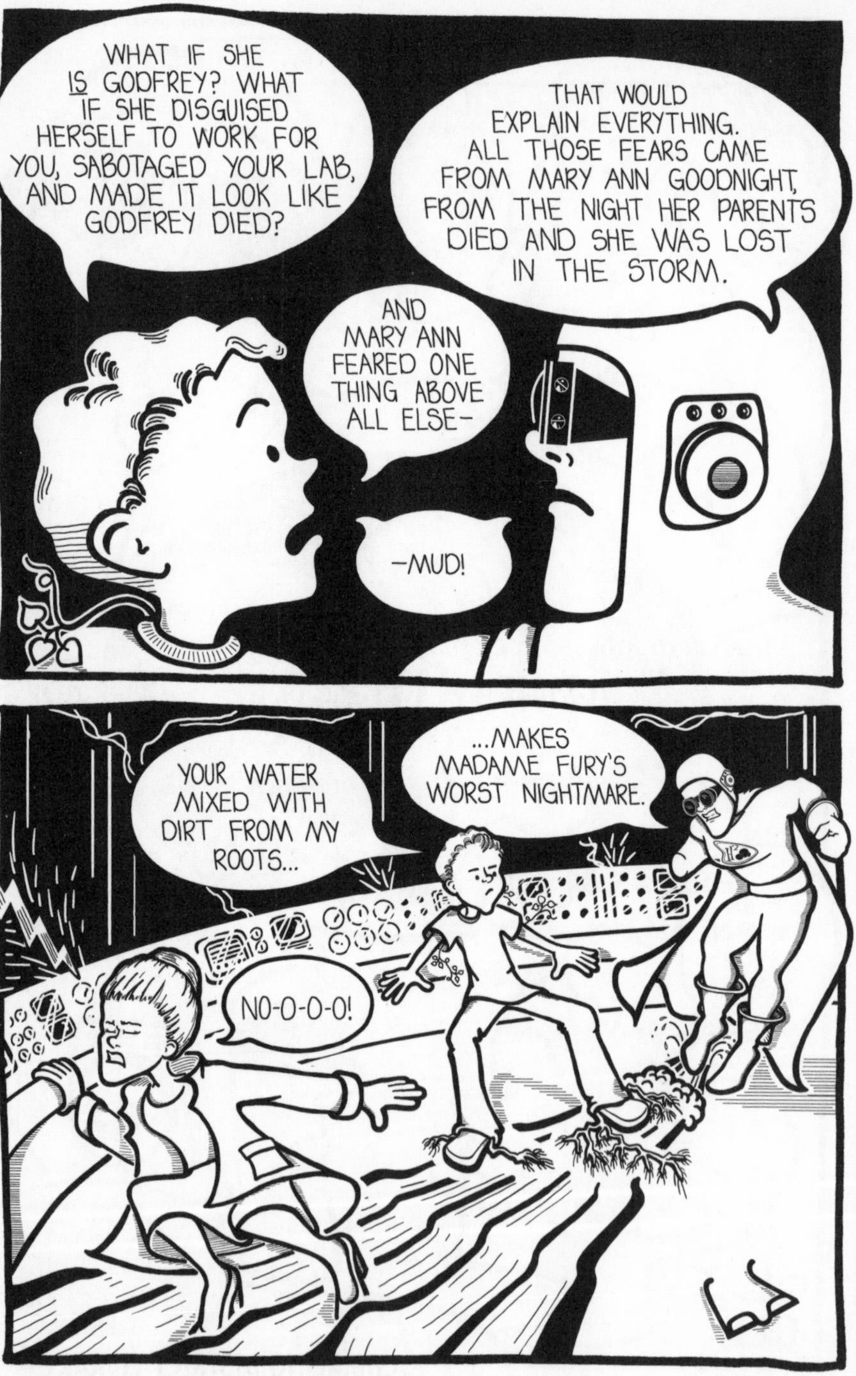
WHAT IF SHE IS GODFREY? WHAT IF SHE DISGUISED HERSELF TO WORK FOR YOU, SABOTAGED YOUR LAB, AND MADE IT LOOK LIKE GODFREY DIED?
THAT WOULD EXPLAIN EVERYTHING. ALL THOSE FEARS CAME FROM MARY ANN GOODNIGHT, FROM THE NIGHT HER PARENTS DIED AND SHE WAS LOST IN THE STORM.
AND MARY ANN FEARED ONE THING ABOVE ALL ELSE-
-MUD!
YOUR WATER MIXED WITH DIRT FROM MY ROOTS...
...MAKES MADAME FURY'S WORST NIGHTMARE.
NO-O-O-O!

thirty-five

I read through Beanboy maybe twenty times.

Either I'd turned him into one of the world's great sidekicks.

Or I'd completely blown any chance to win the contest.

Because here's the thing. I'd just changed H2O's entire official story. He'd been battling evil, protecting the planet, reflecting on the problems of his existence as a freakish, water-logged being through seventy years of comic books.

And I'd just added stuff that hadn't ever been there before.

Me, Tucker MacBean. Who had no business adding anything.

But all the clues were there: The thunderstorm. The fears. Mud. Bugs. Lightning. Even the names: Mary Ann Goodnight. Godfrey Mann. Which were practically the same, only backwards. It all added up. It was almost like the folks who created H2O had planted all this stuff, like bread crumbs in the forest, just waiting for somebody to follow them and figure it out. H2O couldn't. He was too close. It was like his blind spot. He couldn't see that his loyal friend could also be . . . his enemy.

But now, because of a sparkly red dress and a glass of fruit punch, Beanboy *could*.

I stopped.

Beanboy could.

When H2O couldn't, Beanboy could.

I studied my comic book.

Maybe that was the answer.

I'd been searching and drawing and searching some more, for days and weeks, till I'd just about given up. But now, maybe, I'd found it.

All sidekicks needed a few basic traits: Loyalty—check. Courage—no question. Dedication—definitely.

But your contest-winning sidekicks?

They covered the chink.

Superheroes are superheroes for a reason: They're super. Ask Beech. But no matter how super they are, superheroes aren't invincible. A decent superhero always has a chink in the armor: Superman and kryptonite,

Batman and his dark broody spells, Spidey and all that enormous guilt.

H2O and his blind spot.

That's why they need sidekicks. Because your major sidekicks, the great ones, cover the chink. They recognize the kryptonite, the dark spells, the blind spot, then muster all their loyalty, courage, and dedication, recklessly putting themselves in danger, to cover it.

I examined my comic book pages. Maybe that was the answer. Maybe that was Beanboy's heroic heart. Beanboy covered H2O's blind spot. He saw what H2O, through seventy years of comic books, had been too close to see.

It was risky. It could really cheese off the folks at Dark Overlord. It could cost me the contest.

But if Beanboy had taught me anything, it was that you had to do what you thought was right.

And making Beanboy smart enough to figure out Godfrey Mann's secret in time to save H2O seemed . . . right.

Otherwise, he was just a guy with an embarrassing gas problem.

I slid my comic book into the big brown envelope. Started to seal it shut.

Then stopped. I slid the entry form out and gave it a good long look.

And made one small change.

DARK OVERLORD SIDEKICK CONTEST
ENTRY FORM

Name _____ Tucker ~~Mrs.~~ MacBean _____

Address _____ 1801 Polk Street, Wheaton, Kansas _____

    I slid the entry form back into the envelope with my comic book and licked the flap.

thirty-six

And then . . . I began stalking my own mailbox.

Every day I ran home from school, banged it open, and shuffled through the mail, searching for an envelope from Dark Overlord.

Every day I clomped upstairs clutching a handful of envelopes, none of them from Dark Overlord.

The weird thing was, my mom had taken up mail stalking, too. She'd pop in after work, shuffle through the mail, kiss our heads, and dash back out so she wouldn't be late for class.

If I'd gone through with my Desperate Midnight Scheme, she might have found a scholarship with her name on it.

But she wouldn't have kept it.

That's the one thing I hadn't factored into my

equation. Because even if it was wrong for the right reason, even if the reason was so right that the whole thing was only one-sixteenth wrong, my mother would never go for it. She would never take the scholarship. Because my mom was my mom, and she didn't do math with right and wrong.

So no matter how great Beanboy turned out, I couldn't get her a scholarship.

But maybe, possibly, I could get *me* a scholarship. Just like I told her that day on the phone. It wouldn't help her quit her cruddy job, it wouldn't bring her home at night, but it might keep her from worrying so much. It might smooth out that little knot of skin between her eyebrows.

Some things had changed. And some things hadn't.

My dad still lived in Boston.

I got a quick e-mail back from him. Which I kind of wanted to open. And kind of didn't.

I was glad I did.

To: SuperTuck
From: Big Bean in Boston
Re: Birthday Money - Really
Tucker,
Families do need to stick together. I would never be mad
about that. If you want money for your birthday, that's what
I'll send. You can do with it whatever you want.
Dad

Also, even though they were starting to look a little crispy with winter coming on, the spiky orange flowers were still planted in our tire swing.

But I hadn't noticed any more pieces of the MacBean family flying off. Pieces I had to try to catch and put back on.

Sam still babysat Beecher. For two reasons. No, three. Actually, four:

1. I really liked Art Club.
2. I didn't want to quit just because I'd gotten Beanboy finished, especially not after Mrs. Frazee was so nice about letting me join late and use real Bristol board and a non-repro blue pencil.
3. Sam really liked babysitting Beech. (I know. Explain *that*.)
4. Beech screeched and dug his fingernails into my arm every time he thought she wasn't coming back.

Sam didn't pierce me with her Zawicki glare as much, I noticed. She actually talked to me sometimes before snapping her babysitting money from my hand and thumping out the door.

And don't tell anybody this, but once in a while, if her grandpa didn't need her home right away to help with chores, she sort of . . . stayed. And watched cartoons with us. Me and Beech and Sam. She said they didn't get the cartoon channel at their house.

She also said, "Wow. Dillon would love this."

About fifty times.

I don't know if that was a hint or something, but I had to act like I didn't hear it. About fifty times. Because no way was I watching cartoons with Dillon Zawicki.

I mean, things had changed, but not *that* much.

At school, Noah and I still sat at our same lunch table. Sam and Dillon still sat at their table under the EXIT sign. The whole lunch experience was pretty much the same, because, as Noah said, once middle school lunchroom seating patterns are established, they're hard to break.

The Kaleys still shot me down with loser dweeb looks. They shot Sam, too, but they were careful never to do it in front of Emma.

It's not like Emma and Sam were suddenly best friends or anything. But once in a while, if they passed each other in the hall, or if they happened to walk into FACS at the same time, Emma might lift her chin in a casual way and say, "Hey."

At first Sam didn't know how to take it. She'd jerk her head back. Narrow her eyes. Like Emma had slapped her or something. But then I guess she figured out it wasn't a trick. So she started raising her chin in a casual way, too. Not every time. But sometimes.

You really can't underestimate the power of a "hey" from Emma Quinn. It's almost a superpower. Emma's "hey" not only got Sam to lift her chin a little, it pretty much lifted the chin of our whole school. Once Emma started saying "hey" to Sam, other people, here and there, said "hey" to her, too. Not the Kaleys, of course. Or Noah. He was way too nervous. But other people.

And once Sam got used to it (well, as used to it as Sam Zawicki was ever going to get), she started glaring less. She never said "hey" back. But her stomp got a lot softer, which saved a bunch on floor tile. And she must've found a bottle of conditioner somewhere, because her hair didn't stick up quite so much anymore. Sometimes she even braided it, which looked pretty normal.

Once Earhart Middle got used to a kinder, gentler Sam Zawicki, people stopped shrinking away when they saw her. Started walking past her like she was just any other random kid who wasn't planning to hurt them. The whole place seemed less tense.

During an assembly right before Thanksgiving, Mr. Petrucelli said he was proud of the way everyone had been getting along lately.

"And I can pinpoint the exact day things began to change." He was using Coach Wilder's sound system. His voice boomed through the gym. "It was the day an honest, brave young woman came into my office and explained an unfortunate mistake with the FACS room milk. Since that day, Earhart Middle has become a happier, friendlier place to learn, and we have this young womanto thank for that. Let's all give Kaley Crumm a big round of applause."

Everybody clapped. (Okay. Not *everybody.*) Kaley C. stood and waved and smiled and acted like she deserved it.

Oh. One other thing changed. My superpower of invisibility? It sputtered and fizzled till it hardly worked at all. I didn't always stay quiet. I sometimes forgot to stay low. And one day, without thinking about it, I wore a new H2O T-shirt in the magenta color family.

"Dude." Noah stared at it in horror. "What is that?"

"Relax," I said, in a soothing voice. "It's just a shirt."

Yeah. Me. Tucker MacBean. I said, "It's just a shirt."

■ ■ ■

But through it all, I kept checking the mailbox.

And waiting.

thirty-seven

One day when I got home from Art Club, my mom's car was in the driveway.

And our mailbox was empty.

I ran up the stairs. A sweet warm scent drifted over me. I threw open the door and found my mom in the kitchen, frying up pancakes—with blueberry faces—for Beecher and Sam.

Mom was . . . dancing. And singing into the spatula. Something about sitting on a rainbow.

She turned when she heard the door bang open.

"And here he is now," she told the spatula.

Beech bobbed on his chair. "Mom get money." He threw his hands wide. "*Big* money."

I looked at him. Then Mom.

"It *is* pretty big. And it *is* money." She flipped one of the pancakes. "Only better."

She leaned the spatula against the skillet, snatched an envelope from the pile of mail on the counter, and pressed it to her heart.

"You are looking," she said, "at the proud recipient of a full college scholarship." She handed me the envelope.

I stared at it. "A full college scholarship? But—"

Beech pointed at me. "You a guppy." He giggled. "See, Sam? Guppy."

Sam nodded. "He's a guppy, all right."

"And"—Mom scooped a pancake onto a plate and slid it in front of Beech—"I have you to thank for it, Tucker."

Me?

But—

"No," I said. "I changed it. I put *my* name on it."

Mom gave me a funny look.

Sam popped the lid off the syrup. "Maybe you should quit being a Beanboy long enough to read the letter." She squirted Beecher's pancake.

I pulled out the creamy white paper and unfolded it.

Dear Ms. MacBean:

Our committee was moved by your essay about life with your two sons. We were impressed by how you showed that raising a family can be a challenge, but is never a burden.

Never a burden. I read that part again. Never a burden.

With that in mind, we are pleased to award you the Wheaton University
Foundation Single Parent Scholarship.

Single Parent Scholarship?

I looked up. "I don't understand."

"It money." Beech licked syrup off his hand. "*Big*
money."

"It's what you said on the phone, the day we went to
the farmers' market." Mom slid a pancake in front of Sam.
"You told me not to worry about saving for your college.
You said you could get a scholarship. And it clicked in my
head—*I* could get a scholarship. So I did some searching
on the university website—"

"So." I frowned. "That's what you were looking for?
On your laptop?"

She nodded. "It took some digging, but I found this."
She tapped the letter in my hand. "It'll pay for my school
and books, with a little left over. I'll still have to work, but
only part-time. I'll be home every single night with you
guys." She wrapped an arm around Beech's neck and the
other around mine and gave us a squeeze. She kissed the
top of my head and let us go. "You want a pancake? We're
celebrating."

"Um. Sure," I said. "So—"

I looked at the letter. It *was* great news. Mom wouldn't be stuck at her cruddy job all the time. She could go to school during the day, be here at night to order our pizza and make sure Beecher brushed his teeth, and actually get a decent night's sleep once in a while. We'd be able to smell the mango shampoo on her actual hair rather than on a wet towel. It was exactly what I wanted. Exactly what I'd been working for.

Except—

"It's not about the comic book?" I said.

Sam rolled her eyes.

Mom gave me a weird look. "Comic book? No." She poured more batter. The skillet sizzled and popped. "Oh, but you know what? I think you did get something from that comic book place. Black Overcoat?"

"Overlord?" I blinked. "Dark Overlord? I got something from Dark Overlord?"

Mom sorted through the mail and pulled out another envelope.

She handed it to me, and I ran my thumb over it, over the Dark Overlord emblem, red and ominous, the ink raised on the paper.

Probably it wasn't any big deal. Probably it was some kind of form letter. Probably they sent one to everybody who entered their contest, just to tell them they lost.

I slid my finger under the envelope flap. Popped it open. Pulled out the official-looking letter inside. With the official-looking emblem again. And my official name: Tucker MacBean.

I read through it. Quick the first time, then once more to take in all the details.

And I think I really did pass out for a minute, standing right there in the kitchen. The room seemed to tilt, and little spots shimmered around the edges of my vision.

Probably because I'd forgotten to breathe.

"Bad news? Real big bad news?"

I glanced up. Beecher was looking at me, his face scrunched in a frown.

I shook my head. "Good news, Beech. Real big *good* news."

Dear Tucker MacBean:

We at Dark Overlord Comics received thousands of entries to our Sidekick Contest. Many were excellent examples of comic book storytelling and art. Yours, however, was the only entry that truly built on the H2O legend, displaying the innovative spirit that Dark Overlord has always been known for.

We are pleased to name *The Adventures of Beanboy* the winner of the H2O Sidekick Contest. Congratulations and welcome to the Dark Overlord universe.

I stared at the letter.

I hadn't blown it. I hadn't cheesed off the folks at Dark Overlord. I'd changed H2O's official story, added stuff that hadn't been there before. Me, Tucker MacBean, who had no business adding anything. And I hadn't blown it.

I'd won.

As I stood there in the MacBean Family Kitchen, pancakes sizzling and radiator rattling, the letter fluttered in my hands. Fluttered in a steady, rhythmic beat.

But it wasn't just the letter. It was me. It was a beat that came from somewhere inside me, strong, fearless, almost heroic.

I held a hand to my chest.

It was my heart.

That weird heroic beating was . . .

. . . my heart.

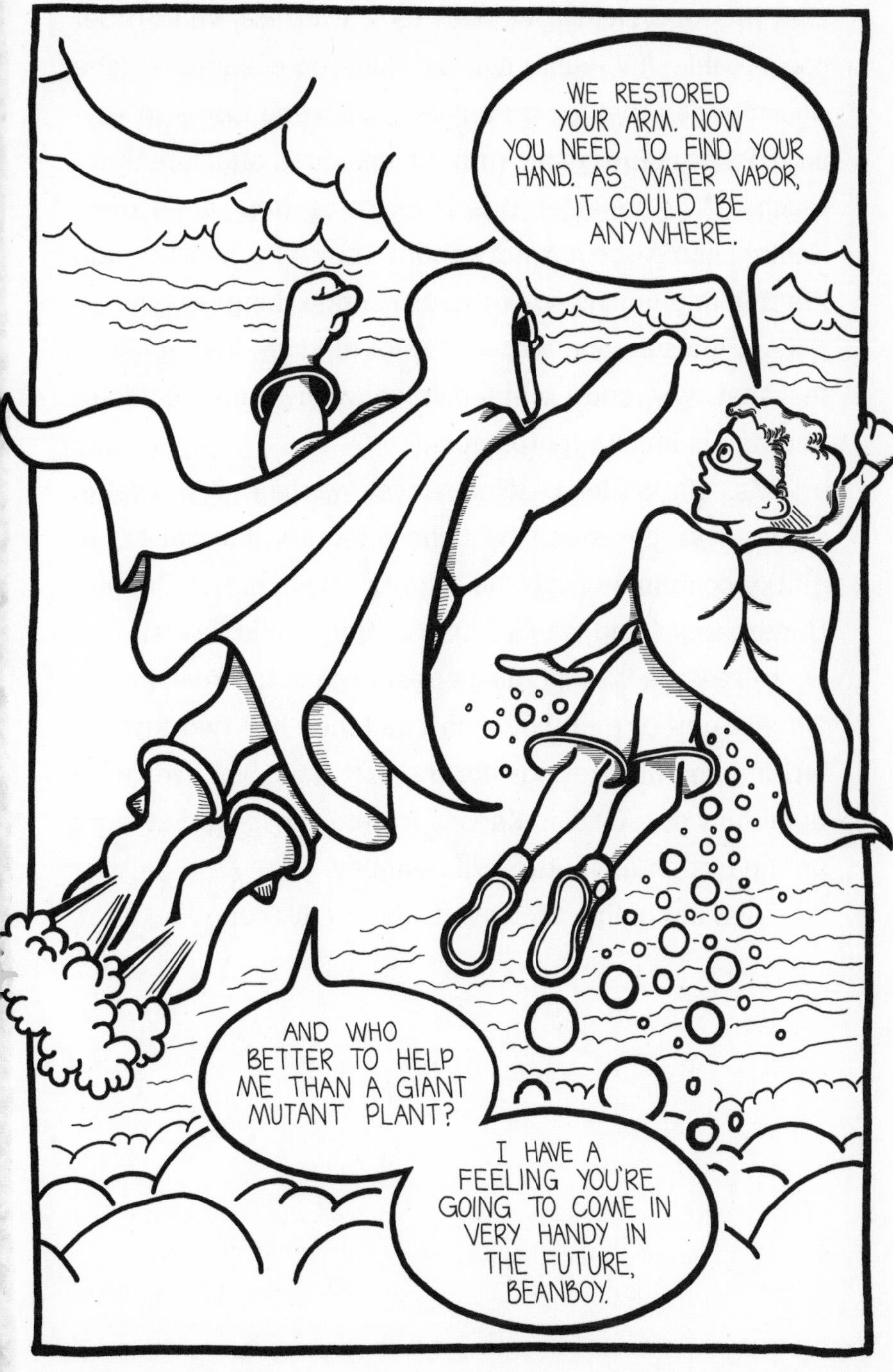
WE RESTORED YOUR ARM. NOW YOU NEED TO FIND YOUR HAND. AS WATER VAPOR, IT COULD BE ANYWHERE.
AND WHO BETTER TO HELP ME THAN A GIANT MUTANT PLANT?
I HAVE A FEELING YOU'RE GOING TO COME IN VERY HANDY IN THE FUTURE, BEANBOY.

LISA HARKRADER has worked as a waitress, short-order cook, cable TV customer service representative (she doesn't wish that job on *anybody*), Marine Corps reservist, UPS package sorter, graphic designer, and substitute teacher. The idea for this book came from a Garrison Keillor Lake Wobegon story about a boy who goes through life thinking he has no power to change things or even to defend himself. She writes: "A lot of kids—and adults— feel that way, and I wanted to show my main character finding his inner superpowers."

Ms. Harkrader's debut novel, *Airball: My Life in Briefs,* was described by School Library Journal as "a quirky combination of The Mighty Ducks meets Captain Underpants," and was a Junior Library Guild Selection as well as a Bank Street College Best Book of the Year. In *The Adventures of Beanboy,* she combines her two loves— writing and illustrating—for the first time. She lives with her family on a farm in Kansas, where she is hard at work on the further adventures of Beanboy.

Visit her online at www.lisaharkrader.com.